Also by Rachael Reed

Sis
Sis 2 Blood on the Streets

Standalone
Codefendant
Codefendant
Once a Cheater
Once a Cheater
Passport Bro
What Happens in Prison
Preference
Sprinkle Sprinkle
Championship Bad
Street Exodus
Street Exodus
Street Royalty
Pawns of Power
SIS
Cartel Bloodline
Get Money Girls
Skip the Games
Til Death Do Us Part

Backpage Hustle
Link in Bio
The Virgin and The Kingpin
A Gangsta's Heart
Boosters
Can't Turn a Hoe Into a Housewife
Better you Than Me
Wig Dealer: How to Start Your wig Business
Trail Ride Blues
Demure Diva
Queen of the Carnival
Caribbean Carnival Hoe

Caribbean
Carnival
Hoe

Caribbean Carnival Hoe

By Rachael Reed

Copyright © 2024 by Rachael Reed

Check Out More Great Products and Free Giveaways
https://tbdbpublishing.com/

Chapter 1: Welcome to the Streets

The streets were alive, pulsing with energy, music thumping through the air as the Carnival roared through the island. Nikki moved like she owned the place, her hips swayin' to the soca beat, skin glistenin' under the Caribbean sun. Her outfit, barely there—gold bikini top, feathers in her hair, glitter across her chest—drew eyes from every direction. Men couldn't help but look, and that's exactly what she wanted.

Nikki wasn't just another girl in the crowd; she was the one everyone knew. Not just for her Carnival looks but for the way she worked the streets. She wasn't shy about it either. They called her a "Carnival Hoe," but to Nikki, that was part of the game. Let 'em think what they want, as long as she got what she needed. And what she needed? Cash, jewels, luxury, and power.

She slid through the crowd like a queen, her eyes scanning for her next mark. It wasn't hard; the Carnival always brought in rich men lookin' for a taste of island life, most of 'em dumb enough to think Nikki was just a pretty face with a wild side. They didn't know she played the game better than they could ever imagine.

Spotting a tall, older man near one of the Carnival trucks, she slowed down, her eyes narrowing. His clothes screamed money, and his thick gold chain and diamond watch were the kind of things that made Nikki's heart race. She licked her lips and strutted toward him, her smile sweet but her mind sharp.

"Yo, you lookin' lost," Nikki said, her voice smooth, flirtatious. She leaned in close enough for him to catch the scent of her perfume, sweet and intoxicating. "Let me show you how we do it on the island."

The man's eyes lit up as he glanced her up and down, clearly takin' the bait. "What's a beautiful woman like you doin' talkin' to a guy like me?" he asked, his voice thick with a foreign accent—New York, maybe.

Nikki flashed him a playful grin, puttin' a hand on his chest. "Oh, baby, you ain't even ready for me."

And just like that, she had him. The way he followed her through the crowd, eyes glued to her like she was his last chance at paradise, Nikki knew he'd be easy. These tourists always were. She led him to a quieter spot, away from the Carnival noise, where the only sounds were the distant drums and their own heavy breathing.

She leaned against the wall, cocking her head as she ran a finger down his chest. "You got somethin' for me?" she purred, eyes glinting with mischief.

The man, already hooked, reached into his pocket and pulled out a stack of cash, fanning it out for her to see. "For you, sweetheart, anything."

Nikki smiled, her hand brushing the money before she slid closer, her lips near his ear. "Mmm, I knew you was different," she whispered, her fingers expertly moving toward his wallet. In a quick motion, she palmed his credit cards, sliding them into her bikini top without him even noticing.

He didn't know it yet, but by the time she was done with him, he'd be callin' his bank, wonderin' where all his money went.

As she led him back to the Carnival crowd, she noticed her homegirl Keisha watchin' from a distance, smirkin' as Nikki worked the guy over. Keisha knew the game well—she and Nikki had been finessin' these streets together for years. Nikki gave her a quick nod, signaling that it was done.

"Yo, Nikki, girl, you really out here hustlin'," Keisha laughed as Nikki strolled over, the man long gone back into the drunken masses.

"You know how it is," Nikki replied, twirling the stolen credit cards between her fingers before tucking them into her waistband. "They always fall for it. These fools don't know nothin' about the real grind."

Keisha nodded, her eyes scanning the crowd for their next play. "But, for real, sis, you gotta be careful. Word on the street is some of these guys ain't playin'. You run into the wrong one, and it's over."

Nikki rolled her eyes, tossin' her long, curly hair over her shoulder. "Ain't nobody out here gon' touch me. I run this shit. The only thing these men gon' do is hand me their cash and walk away broke."

Keisha snorted, shaking her head. "You wild, girl. But hey, I'm just sayin'... you know how fast things change out here. It only take one wrong move."

Nikki shrugged, but she knew Keisha wasn't wrong. The streets were unforgiving. She'd grown up in them, learned the hard way how to survive. There was always someone lurkin', waitin' to take what you had. But Nikki? She'd made a name for herself. She was known as the one who always got away, who always stayed one step ahead.

As the day faded into night, the streets got wilder. Music blasted louder, the smell of jerk chicken and sweat filled the air, and the Carnival crowd only grew more intense. Nikki loved it—the chaos, the energy. It was her world, and she knew how to thrive in it.

Later that night, she met up with Keisha at one of the local clubs. It was packed, and the bass vibrated through her chest as they made their way to the bar. The drinks were flowing, the lights flashing, and Nikki felt invincible.

But in the back of her mind, there was always that voice—Keisha's warning. She knew it could all come crashing down if she made the wrong move. But that was the risk. And Nikki wasn't afraid of the game. She thrived off it.

As the night wore on, a man caught her eye. He was posted up in a corner, watching her with an intensity that sent a shiver down her spine. He was tall, dark, and dangerous-looking, with diamond-studded earrings and a gold chain thick enough to choke someone. She didn't recognize him, but he had the kind of presence that couldn't be ignored.

Keisha nudged her, noticing her stare. "Yo, who's that? You know him?"

Nikki shook her head. "Nah, but I got a feelin' I'm about to."

Before she could second-guess herself, she sauntered over, her hips swayin' to the beat. She had no idea who he was, but Nikki knew how to play her cards. She wasn't just any girl, and whoever he was, he was about to find that out.

She stopped in front of him, flashing a confident smirk. "You lookin' for somethin'?"

He raised an eyebrow, his gaze sweeping over her before a slow smile spread across his face. "Maybe I am. What you got?"

Nikki's heart raced, but she kept her cool. "Depends on what you're willin' to give."

The man leaned closer, his voice low and dangerous. "I'm willing to give a lot, baby girl. But just know, once you in, you ain't gettin' out."

Something about the way he said it made Nikki's stomach twist, but she pushed the feeling aside. She wasn't scared. She could handle him.

"I guess we'll see about that," she replied, her smile never wavering.

The night continued, the drinks flowed, and Nikki found herself drawn deeper into conversation with the mysterious man. She didn't know it then, but this was the moment everything would change. This wasn't just another mark, and this game wasn't like the others.

As the club lights flashed and the music pounded, Nikki felt the weight of something bigger than herself closing in. But for now, all she could do was ride the wave.

Because in the streets, you didn't stop. You didn't back down. And for Nikki, there was no turning back.

Chapter 2: The Hustle

The hot Caribbean sun beat down on the streets, the scent of grilled jerk chicken and rum punch fillin' the air. Carnival was still in full swing, with music blarin' and people dancin' like there was no tomorrow. Nikki stood on the edge of the crowd, her sharp eyes scanning the scene, searchin' for her next score. She had already hustled a few small-timers since last night, but she was lookin' for somethin' bigger. Someone with real money. She wasn't out here for no pocket change—she wanted that serious cash.

Her gaze landed on him: an older man standin' near a tourist bus, his hand grippin' the handle of a leather briefcase. He was in his fifties, maybe sixties, wearin' a crisp linen shirt and gold-rimmed sunglasses that screamed wealth. His pale skin glistened with sweat, clearly not used to the Caribbean heat. Out of place, out of his element. Perfect.

"Look at this fool," Nikki muttered to herself with a smirk. "He about to learn how we do it on these streets."

With a flick of her hair, Nikki slid into action, swayin' her hips as she walked toward him. Her bikini top barely covered her, and the colorful beads that hung around her waist jingled with every step. The tourists here ate that up—the island fantasy. And Nikki knew how to sell it.

"Excuse me," she called out, feignin' innocence, her accent thick and sultry. "You lookin' lost, papi. You need some help?"

The man's head snapped up, and as soon as his eyes landed on her, Nikki knew she had him. His gaze drifted down her body, lingerin' on her chest before he quickly tried to play it off, clearin' his throat.

"Uh, yes. I mean, no... I'm just—" He fumbled with his words, clearly flustered, and Nikki stepped closer, lettin' her hand brush against his arm.

"Ain't no need to be nervous, baby," she purred, her lips curlin' into a smile. "I just wanna make sure you enjoyin' yourself. You don't wanna be all alone, do you?"

His hesitation melted away as Nikki leaned in closer, her perfume hittin' his nose, a mix of sweet coconut and spice. She could see the wheels turnin' in his head, and she already knew where this was goin'.

"I could use some company," he finally said, his voice low and suggestive.

Nikki smiled, her eyes flashin' with that seductive charm she had perfected over the years. "Well, you just found the best company on the island."

They spent the rest of the afternoon together, Nikki layin' it on thick, gigglin' at his corny jokes, touchin' his arm whenever she had the chance. She kept his drink filled, makin' sure he was buzzed but still clear-headed enough to follow her lead. She had him eatin' outta her hand in no time.

As the sun began to set, Nikki suggested they go back to his hotel. "We could have a little more fun, away from all these crowds," she whispered, runnin' her fingers through his thinning hair. He didn't even hesitate, already reachin' for his wallet to pay their tab. Nikki's eyes flickered to the fat stack of cash he pulled out, and she licked her lips. This was about to be too easy.

The hotel was one of the fancier ones, the kind only tourists and businesspeople with deep pockets could afford. As they walked into the lavish lobby, the older man smiled down at her, obviously thinkin' he'd scored. Little did he know, he was the one about to get played.

Once inside his room, Nikki made her move. She slipped out of her sandals and strolled toward the balcony, lettin' the breeze hit her skin. She knew he was watchin', and when she turned around, she gave him a slow, seductive smile. "You got any champagne in here?" she asked, her voice low, teasing.

"Of course," he said eagerly, movin' toward the minibar. As soon as he turned his back, Nikki's eyes darted to the leather briefcase he had dropped by the bed. Without hesitating, she moved toward it, her fingers workin' quickly to pop the latch open.

Inside was exactly what she was hopin' for—wads of cash, neatly stacked. There was also a velvet case that, when she opened it, revealed a diamond necklace that sparkled under the soft light of the hotel room. Nikki's heart raced. This was it. She was about to come up big.

But just as she was about to grab the cash, she heard the man's voice behind her. "You find what you're lookin' for?"

Her blood ran cold, but Nikki was quick on her feet. She turned, flashin' a sly grin as she held up the diamond necklace. "I was just admirin' this. You buy it for someone special?"

The man smirked, steppin' closer. "Maybe I'll buy it for you."

Nikki tilted her head, playin' along. "Mmm, that's sweet. But you know, I think I deserve somethin' more... personal."

She stepped closer to him, lettin' her hand trail down his chest. His breath hitched, and Nikki saw her moment. In one swift move, she spun him around, pushin' him onto the bed. Before he could react, she was straddlin' him, her hand coverin' his mouth.

"Don't move," she whispered, her voice now deadly serious. "You make a sound, and I swear to God, you won't leave this room."

His eyes widened in panic, and Nikki could feel his pulse racin' beneath her fingers. She smiled, leanin' down so her lips were near his ear. "You just got played, old man."

With that, she grabbed the cash, stuffin' it into her purse along with the diamond necklace. She kept her eyes on him the whole time, makin' sure he didn't try to get brave. Once she had what she needed, she stood up, flashin' him one last cold smile.

"You might wanna rethink comin' back to the island after this," she said as she slipped out the door, leavin' him frozen on the bed, too scared to even move.

As soon as Nikki stepped outta the hotel, she could feel the adrenaline pumpin' through her veins. The streetlights flickered above, and the sound of soca music drifted from the distance, but all she could focus on was the fat stack of cash she had just scored. She had pulled it off, once again. No one could touch her. She was untouchable.

Walkin' through the streets, she could feel the weight of the diamond necklace in her purse, its cold metal remindin' her of her success. She felt invincible. Nikki thrived on this—doin' what she had to, runnin' the game, and gettin' what was hers.

By the time she met back up with Keisha, her best friend was already waitin' at their usual spot near the corner of the block. Keisha's eyes widened when she saw the grin on Nikki's face. "Girl, don't tell me you just hit another lick."

Nikki pulled out the cash and flashed it at Keisha with a triumphant smirk. "Hell yeah. And this one was sweet. Got me a lil' somethin' extra too."

Keisha laughed, shakin' her head. "Girl, you wild. But you better be careful. One of these days, somebody gon' catch on."

Nikki rolled her eyes, already plannin' her next move. "Please. I ain't worried 'bout none of these fools. They never see me comin'. I got this on lock."

As the night carried on, Nikki felt untouchable, like she could hustle her way outta anything. But deep down, somethin' gnawed at her—Keisha's words echoing in her mind. One of these days, somebody gon' catch on.

But tonight wasn't that night. Not yet. And Nikki wasn't gonna stop until she had everything she wanted.

The streets were her playground, and Nikki was just gettin' started.

Chapter 3: Gossip in the Streets

The streets was always talkin', always buzzing with rumors, stories, and gossip that spread like wildfire. And right now, it was all about Nikki. Her name was on everybody's lips—men, women, and even the old heads who hung out on the corner, watchin' everything go down.

"Yo, you hear 'bout that chick Nikki? She out here finessin' dudes left and right," one man said, leanin' against a busted-up car, takin' a long drag from his cigarette.

"Yeah, man," his friend replied, shakin' his head. "She wild, bruh. I heard she took some old head for everything. Man ain't even know what hit him."

They laughed, the sound carryin' through the humid night air. It was the same everywhere Nikki went—the whispers, the looks, the low conversations that stopped the moment she walked by. She wasn't just another girl on the block anymore; she was the girl everyone was talkin' about.

Nikki knew it too. She could feel the eyes on her every time she strutted through the streets, her head held high, her hips swayin' like she owned the damn place. She thrived on it. The envy, the admiration, the respect—it fueled her. The men who warned each other to be careful around her, the women who shot jealous looks when they saw her drippin' in new jewelry or ridin' in some man's luxury car—it all made her feel powerful. Untouchable.

"Girl, they really out here talkin' 'bout you," Keisha said one day as they walked down the block, the sun blazin' overhead. "Like, everywhere I go, it's Nikki this, Nikki that. You got these girls heated."

Nikki smirked, adjustin' her shades as they passed a group of women on the corner, all of 'em shootin' daggers with their eyes. "Let 'em talk. I must be doin' somethin' right if they hatin' this hard."

Keisha shrugged, her expression neutral, but Nikki caught the way her friend's eyes narrowed as they passed by another group of men, whisperin' low and chucklin' when they saw Nikki.

"Yo, that's the chick right there," one of them muttered. "She the one who got ol' boy for like five racks."

"Damn, for real? She cold as ice," another one replied, his eyes followin' Nikki's every step.

Keisha glanced at Nikki, her tone lower now. "But for real, Nikki... you gotta be careful. The streets talkin', and you know what that means. These dudes ain't stupid forever. Somebody gonna figure out what you doin'. Ain't nobody gon' let you play 'em like that without some kinda payback."

Nikki waved her off, not even breakin' her stride. "Please. These fools ain't ready for me. They all think they different, think they special. But they all the same—lookin' for somethin' they can't handle."

Keisha sighed, clearly not convinced, but she let it go. Nikki was always like this—reckless, fearless, confident. But Keisha had seen enough to know the streets were never as simple as people thought. There was always someone watchin', someone waitin' for you to slip.

Later that night, they hit up a local club, the kind where the music was loud, the lights were low, and the air was thick with smoke. Nikki walked in like she owned the place, her head high, her dress tight, and her heels clickin' against the worn-out floor. Heads turned, eyes locked on her as she made her way to the bar, Keisha in tow.

It didn't take long before some dude slid up beside her, flashin' a grin and showin' off the gold watch on his wrist. "You lookin' for company, baby?" he asked, his voice smooth like he thought he had game.

Nikki didn't even look at him, just sipped her drink and smirked. "Depends. You got somethin' worth my time?"

The man chuckled, clearly thinkin' he was the one. "Oh, trust me. I got more than you can handle."

Nikki finally turned her head, givin' him a once-over. He was flashy, definitely had money, but there was somethin' about him that felt off. Maybe it was the way he was too eager, or maybe it was the fact that she'd seen him talkin' to the same girls outside earlier. Either way, she wasn't interested.

"You cute," she said, her tone dismissive, "but I ain't lookin' for no small-time hustler tonight."

His face fell, but Nikki didn't care. She wasn't about to waste her time on some two-bit player tryin' to impress her with a watch he probably couldn't even afford.

Keisha laughed as the guy walked away, lookin' embarrassed. "Damn, girl, you really lettin' these dudes have it."

Nikki shrugged, takin' another sip of her drink. "Ain't no point in playin' with scrubs. I need someone who can match my hustle."

But as the night went on, Keisha's words kept echoing in Nikki's mind. The streets were talkin', and while she loved the attention, there was a part of her that couldn't shake the feelin' that maybe she was flyin' too close to the sun.

"Girl, you ain't worried 'bout nothin'?" Keisha asked as they sat at the bar, her eyes dartin' around the room. "I mean, all these dudes you playin'? One of 'em gonna catch feelings, and when they do, it ain't gonna be pretty."

Nikki leaned back in her chair, her eyes cold, calculatin'. "Ain't nobody catchin' nothin' but an L if they try me. I know these streets better than they do. They think they runnin' game? Nah, I'm runnin' it."

But even as she said it, Nikki couldn't help but notice the way the bartender looked at her, the way the other girls in the club whispered and glanced in her direction. Her name was spreadin', her hustle was growin', and the streets was payin' attention.

The next day, Nikki walked down the block, her new diamond necklace glistenin' in the sunlight. She felt good, like she was untouchable. But as she turned the corner, she overheard a conversation that stopped her in her tracks.

"Yo, I heard Nikki got somethin' big planned. She really out here finessin' dudes like it's nothin'. I wouldn't be surprised if somebody put a hit on her ass."

Nikki froze for a second, her heart poundin' in her chest. A hit? Nah, they were just talkin'. People always talked. But the way they said it, like it was real, sent a chill down her spine.

She kept walkin', tryin' to shake off the feelin', but it stuck with her. She had always brushed off the rumors, the gossip, the warnings. She saw them as proof that she was makin' moves, that she was the queen of this game. But now? Now she wasn't so sure.

Later that night, Keisha showed up at Nikki's apartment, her face serious. "Girl, we need to talk."

Nikki raised an eyebrow, still feelin' the adrenaline from her latest hustle. "What now? More people talkin'?"

Keisha sat down, lookin' dead serious. "It ain't just talk no more, Nikki. I'm hearin' some real threats. These dudes don't like gettin' played, and they lookin' for you."

Nikki smirked, but there was a flicker of doubt in her eyes. "Please. They just mad 'cause they got finessed. Ain't nobody doin' nothin'."

Keisha leaned forward, her voice low. "You keep thinkin' that, girl, but I'm tellin' you, the streets is watchin'. And when they come for you, you ain't gonna see it comin'."

For the first time, Nikki felt the weight of her choices pressin' down on her. She had always been in control, always one step ahead. But now? Now it felt like the streets were catchin' up to her.

She looked out the window, her mind racin', the sound of distant sirens echoing through the night. The game was changin', and Nikki wasn't sure if she was ready for what came next.

But one thing was for sure—she wasn't backin' down.

Not yet.

Chapter 4: Trouble Brews

The bass pounded through the walls of the packed club, lights flashin' overhead like fireworks, casting shadows on the crowd. Nikki stood at the bar, sippin' on her rum punch, her eyes scanning the room for her next play. The night was young, and she was in her zone, feelin' herself. She loved the energy of the spot—sweaty bodies grinding on the dance floor, the smell of liquor and smoke thick in the air. It was where she thrived.

But tonight wasn't just any night. She could feel somethin' different in the air, a tension that made the hairs on the back of her neck stand up.

Keisha leaned in close, yelling over the music, "Yo, you see that dude over there? He's been eyein' you since we walked in. That boy look like money."

Nikki turned, casually glancing toward the back of the room. Her eyes landed on him. He was posted up by the VIP section, surrounded by a group of his boys. He had the look—slick, dangerous, and drippin' in gold. He wore a fresh white tee, gold chain heavy on his neck, diamonds in his ears, and a smirk that said he knew he ran shit.

Rome.

The name rolled through the crowd like a whispered warning. Nikki knew who he was. Everybody knew Rome. He wasn't just some dealer; he was one of the most connected dudes in the streets, pushin' weight and runnin' the game. Word was, if you crossed Rome, you wouldn't live to regret it.

Nikki wasn't scared, though. She liked playin' with fire. And Rome? He was definitely fire.

"He cute," Nikki said with a smirk, pretending not to be fazed, but she felt that magnetic pull between them even from across the room. There was somethin' dangerous about him, somethin' that told her messin' with him could bring more trouble than she wanted. But that didn't stop her.

Rome locked eyes with her, and it felt like the whole club disappeared for a second. His gaze was intense, almost predatory. Nikki swallowed her drink, cool as ever, but her heart was beatin' faster.

Keisha nudged her. "Girl, be careful. That ain't no regular dude."

Nikki shrugged, still starin' at him. "Ain't no man regular around me, Keish. He look like he ready to spend, and I ain't about to miss my shot."

Before Keisha could respond, Rome started walkin' toward them, pushin' through the crowd like the king he thought he was. His boys fell back, lettin' him handle his business. The closer he got, the more Nikki felt the heat between them buildin'. There was no denyin' the chemistry.

Rome stepped up, leanin' on the bar beside her, his cologne strong, mixin' with the smoke and sweat. He looked her up and down, takin' his time before speakin'.

"What's good, ma?" His voice was smooth, deep, and full of confidence.

Nikki turned to face him, keepin' her cool, even though his presence had her insides twisted. "Chillin'. You?"

Rome chuckled, his eyes not leavin' hers. "I'm better now. I been watchin' you all night. You the baddest one in here."

Nikki smirked, takin' a sip from her glass. "I know."

Rome raised an eyebrow, likin' her boldness. Most girls would've been tryna impress him, but not Nikki. She wasn't about to let him think he had her like that. She could play this game too.

"You got a name?" he asked, his voice low and dangerous.

"Nikki," she said, lockin' eyes with him. "You?"

He leaned in closer, his breath warm against her ear. "Rome."

She already knew that, but she let him think she didn't. She liked playin' dumb, makin' them think they had the upper hand. Meanwhile, she was always two steps ahead.

"I heard about you, Rome," Nikki said, her tone flirtatious but cautious. "They say you run these streets."

Rome chuckled, his lips curlin' into a grin. "I run more than just these streets, baby. But let's not talk 'bout that. I came over here to see if you tryna ride with a real one."

Nikki felt her pulse quicken, the danger of it all makin' her blood race. She knew messin' with Rome could bring complications—he wasn't the type you just walked away from. But at the same time, she couldn't help but feel drawn to him. His power, his confidence... it was magnetic.

"Maybe I am," she said, leanin' in closer, their lips almost touchin'. "But what's in it for me?"

Rome smirked, reachin' into his pocket and pullin' out a wad of cash. He fanned it out, his eyes never leavin' hers. "I take care of what's mine, Nikki. You roll with me, you ain't never gon' want for nothin'."

Nikki felt the heat rise in her chest. She knew better than to trust a man like him. But the allure was there. The money, the power, the thrill of the danger—it was like a drug, and she was already addicted.

"I'm not lookin' to be anyone's," she said, her voice low and smooth, but Rome's grin only widened.

"We'll see about that," he said, puttin' the cash back in his pocket. "Come with me. Let's talk somewhere quieter."

Keisha shot her a look, a silent warning. But Nikki didn't care. She was too far gone now. She nodded to Rome, feelin' the rush of the decision. She followed him through the crowd, her heart poundin', adrenaline pumpin' through her veins.

They stepped outside, into the humid night, where the streetlights flickered dimly over the cracked pavement. Rome led her to a sleek black car parked on the curb. The driver, a thick dude in a suit, opened the door, and Nikki slid inside, Rome close behind.

As they drove through the city, the streets blurrin' past, Nikki felt the weight of his gaze on her. He was studyin' her, like he was tryin' to figure her out. She didn't like it. She preferred to be the one with the upper hand. But with Rome, that was gonna be harder than usual.

"You different," he said finally, breakin' the silence. "Most chicks fall all over themselves tryna get my attention. You? You actin' like you runnin' game on me."

Nikki smiled, glancin' at him from the corner of her eye. "Maybe I am."

Rome leaned back in his seat, a slow grin spreadin' across his face. "I like that. But don't get it twisted, ma. You ain't runnin' nothin' here. You roll with me, you play by my rules."

Nikki's guard went up. She didn't like the way he said that, like she was already his. But at the same time, there was somethin' about him that kept her interested. She couldn't walk away, not yet.

"We'll see who's runnin' what," she said, her voice defiant, but inside, she felt the pull of somethin' darker, somethin' dangerous.

They pulled up to a penthouse downtown, the kind that overlooked the whole city. Rome got out, openin' the door for her like a gentleman, but Nikki knew better. He wasn't no gentleman. He was a shark, circlin', waitin' to take a bite.

As they stepped inside the lavish apartment, Nikki took in the luxury—plush furniture, marble floors, floor-to-ceiling windows that showed the lights of the city below. This was Rome's world, and she was just a visitor.

Rome handed her a glass of champagne, his eyes still fixed on her. "So, what's it gonna be, Nikki? You rollin' with me or not?"

Nikki hesitated, feelin' the weight of the decision hangin' in the air. This was bigger than any con she'd run before. Rome wasn't like the other men she finessed. He was dangerous, powerful, and once she was in, there'd be no gettin' out.

But that's what made it so tempting. The risk, the thrill. She couldn't resist.

"I'm in," she said, takin' a sip of the champagne.

Rome smiled, his eyes gleamin' with satisfaction. "Good. But remember, Nikki—once you in, there's no goin' back."

Nikki felt the weight of his words settle on her chest. Trouble was brewin', and she knew it. But for now, she was playin' the game, and she wasn't about to back down.

Chapter 5: Crossing Lines

Nikki's life had turned into a fast-moving blur of luxury, chaos, and cash. Every day brought something new—gifts, money, trips, and promises of more to come. Rome was pourin' it all on thick. From designer clothes to five-star hotels, Nikki was livin' the kind of life she'd only dreamed about.

At first, she was ridin' high on the excitement. The trips to Miami, Jamaica, and anywhere Rome wanted to flex—private jets, bottles poppin' at every club, and VIP sections filled with celebrities. She had gone from hustlin' on the streets to livin' like royalty, and for a minute, she thought she could handle it all.

But as the weeks went by, Rome started askin' for more than just her presence on his arm. He wanted her involved, not just as eye candy, but as a player in his business. And his business? It was dirty.

"Yo, Nikki," Rome said one night, leanin' back in the leather seat of the Bentley he'd just gifted her. "I got this move I'm makin' at one of these upscale parties tomorrow night. Some of these rich cats don't wanna deal with the usual street dudes, you feel me? But you... you could slide in smooth, and they'd never see it comin'."

Nikki tensed. She knew what Rome was hintin' at. She'd been around him long enough to understand the game he was runnin'—pushin' product, movin' weight. At the start, she had kept her distance, makin' it clear she wasn't tryin' to get involved in that side of his hustle. But now? He was pullin' her deeper, and it was gettin' harder to say no.

Rome's hand slid across her thigh, his voice low and smooth. "Come on, baby. You know you got that charm, that look. All you gotta do is show up, smile, and collect the bag. That's it. It's easy."

Easy. That's what they all said when they were tryin' to drag you into somethin' foul. Nikki hesitated, lookin' out the window as the city lights flashed by. Part of her wanted to walk away, keep it movin' before she crossed a line she couldn't come back from. But another part of her, the part that craved that fast money and the rush of power, was tempted.

"Rome..." she started, but he cut her off.

"Nah, don't act scared now," he said, his voice a little sharper. "You livin' this life, right? I'm takin' care of you, showin' you things these other dudes couldn't even dream of. It's time you put in some work."

Nikki bit her lip, feelin' the pressure buildin'. She had played her fair share of games with men, but this was different. This was dangerous. Still, the allure of the money, the lifestyle, the power—it was hard to resist.

Finally, she nodded, her voice steady. "Aight. I'll do it."

Rome smiled, that predatory gleam flashin' in his eyes. "That's my girl."

The next night, Nikki stepped into the high-end party, feelin' like she was walkin' into a whole new world. The mansion was packed with people—rich men in expensive suits, women drippin' in diamonds, and enough champagne to fill a pool. The atmosphere buzzed with luxury, but beneath it all was that unspoken understanding. Everyone here was dirty, just like the streets she came from, only they wore their filth under a thin layer of class.

Nikki moved through the crowd, her eyes sharp, her heart poundin'. She knew what she had to do. Rome had already set it up. She was there to be seen, to flirt, to make these rich men feel like they were special. But in reality, she was playin' them, all while movin' Rome's product under their noses.

Her target was some businessman, older, with gray hair and the kind of arrogance that came with too much money. He was sittin' in a corner, drinkin' expensive whiskey, and from the way his eyes lit up when he saw her, Nikki knew this would be easy.

She slid up to him, her smile sweet and dangerous, her voice soft as she leaned in. "Mind if I join you?"

The man grinned, already caught in her web. "Not at all. What's a beautiful woman like you doin' here alone?"

Nikki laughed lightly, brushin' her hand against his arm. "Just lookin' for some fun, maybe a lil' business too. You look like the kind of man who knows how to handle both."

The man's grin widened, and Nikki played her role perfectly. She flirted, made small talk, made him feel like he was in control. But all the while, she was watchin', waitin' for the moment to make the exchange.

Rome had set it up so clean—Nikki didn't even have to touch the product. She just had to be the distraction, keep the man's attention on her while Rome's people handled the rest. It was smooth, quick, and when it was over, Nikki walked out of that mansion with a fat stack of cash and a sense of unease settlin' in her chest.

The money was flowin' faster than ever after that. Rome kept Nikki busy, pullin' her into more deals, more parties, more dangerous situations. He showered her with gifts—new cars, jewelry, trips to the most exotic places—but every time he handed her another expensive present, Nikki felt the weight of her decisions growin' heavier.

She was in it now, and it was too late to back out.

One night, after yet another high-end party, Nikki sat in the back of the Bentley Rome had given her, starin' out at the city streets. Her phone buzzed, and when she looked down, she saw a message from Keisha.

Keisha: "Girl, where you at? Haven't seen you in a minute."

Nikki hesitated before replyin'. She hadn't been around Keisha much since she'd started runnin' with Rome. Keisha had warned her, told her to be careful, but Nikki didn't listen. Now? She wasn't sure if she even could explain what her life had become.

Nikki: "I'm good. Just busy."

Keisha's reply was immediate.

Keisha: "Busy doin' what? You better not be out here in some mess, Nikki. You know how these dudes play."

Nikki sighed, her fingers hoverin' over the screen. She wanted to tell Keisha the truth, tell her how deep she was in, how she was losin' control. But instead, she typed:

Nikki: "Don't worry 'bout me. I got this."

But deep down, she wasn't sure if she did.

Days turned into weeks, and the lines between Nikki's life as a con artist and her new role in Rome's drug game blurred. She was movin' weight now, even if she wasn't the one holdin' the product. She was involved, and with every deal, every party, every time she smiled at another rich mark and played her part, she felt herself sinkin' deeper.

The fast money had a hold on her. The thrill of the hustle, the power she felt walkin' into a room and commandin' attention—it was addictive. But the deeper she got, the more dangerous it became.

One night, after a particularly tense party, Rome slid up beside her, handin' her another wad of cash. "You're good at this, baby. I knew you would be. We about to make some real money."

Nikki took the cash, but her hand trembled. She was in too deep now. She could feel it. The streets were startin' to close in, and she knew it was only a matter of time before it all came crashin' down.

She just didn't know when. Or how bad it would be.

The game was gettin' real. And Nikki was about to find out just how dangerous it could get.

Chapter 6: The Crime Boss's Obsession

The night was heavy with the scent of sea air, minglin' with smoke and the faint echo of music driftin' from the Carnival down the street. Nikki was perched in the back of Rome's latest ride, a sleek black Range Rover, watchin' the lights flicker over the narrow, worn streets as they passed. She was nervous, though she'd never let it show. She kept her game face on, the same one she always wore when she had to play cool in the middle of somethin' bigger than herself.

Tonight was different. Rome had been talkin' all day about a meetin'. Not with his usual crew—this one was with *him.* The man who controlled everything behind the scenes. Vicente.

Nikki had heard his name whispered in the streets, like he was some sort of legend. A crime boss straight outta the Caribbean underworld. Ruthless, cold, and dangerous as hell. They said he ran things from the islands to Miami, from the drugs to the guns, and everything in between. Rome wasn't nothin' compared to Vicente, and that alone made Nikki's chest tighten.

"Relax, baby," Rome said, glancin' at her from the driver's seat, his voice smooth but with an edge. "Vicente ain't the type to do small talk, but he gonna like you. Just be you, and everything will go smooth."

Nikki forced a smile, leanin' back into the leather seat, feelin' that chill creepin' up her spine. "I'm good, Rome. Don't worry 'bout me."

Rome chuckled, his hand reachin' over to rest on her thigh. "You always good, Nikki. That's why you ridin' with me."

But Nikki wasn't sure. She had learned by now that ridin' with Rome meant dealin' with more than just money and fancy trips. It meant dealin' with men like Vicente, and somethin' told her she wasn't ready for this. Not tonight.

They pulled up to a gated estate, the kind that screamed money and power. The security guard barely glanced at them before lettin' them in, and as the gate swung open, Nikki caught sight of the mansion in the distance. It was massive, sittin' on a cliff overlookin' the sea, with lights spillin' out from every window. The kind of place that looked beautiful but dangerous, like it could swallow you whole if you let it.

Rome parked, and they stepped out, the warm Caribbean breeze hittin' her skin. Nikki fixed her hair, glancin' at Rome. "So, what's the deal? We here for business or pleasure?"

Rome smirked. "With Vicente, it's always business. But don't worry—he just wanna meet you. He's been askin' about you."

Nikki's stomach dropped at those words. *Askin' about her?* Why? What did he know?

Before she could ask more, they were led inside by one of Vicente's men, a tall, silent figure who barely acknowledged their presence. Nikki felt the tension in the air as they stepped into the grand living room. The place was immaculate—marble floors, expensive artwork, and a massive glass wall that overlooked the sea.

And there, loungin' on a plush leather couch, was Vicente.

He was older than she expected, maybe in his late forties, but he had the look of a man who had seen and done too much. His skin was dark, his eyes cold and calculatin', and the way he watched her as they entered the room sent a shiver through her. He was dressed in all white, casual but sharp, like he didn't need to try to prove his power.

"Rome," Vicente said, his voice deep, accented, commandin'. "You brought her."

Rome nodded, his usual swagger intact. "This is Nikki. The one I've been tellin' you about."

Vicente's eyes didn't leave hers. He didn't even blink. Nikki felt like she was standin' in front of a predator, and every instinct told her to be careful. This wasn't some random street dude. This was a man who could end her with one word.

"Nikki," Vicente said, his voice smooth but laced with somethin' dark. "I've heard a lot about you."

Nikki kept her expression neutral, though her heart was racin'. "All good things, I hope."

Vicente smiled, but it didn't reach his eyes. "Of course. You've impressed Rome, and that's not easy. He speaks highly of you."

Rome chuckled, but Nikki could barely focus. Vicente's gaze was too intense, too direct. She felt like he was dissectin' her, tryin' to figure out every secret she had without her sayin' a word.

"You got somethin' special, Nikki," Vicente continued, standin' up slowly, his eyes never leavin' hers. "The kind of presence that makes people notice. And I like people who can make others notice."

Nikki shifted slightly, her nerves on edge. She wasn't sure what Vicente was gettin' at, but she didn't like the way he was lookin' at her. It wasn't the same as Rome, who wanted to possess her. Vicente? He was different. It felt like he wanted somethin' more, somethin' darker.

Rome stepped forward, breakin' the tension. "Vicente, I told you she was the real deal. We been makin' moves together, and everything's been clean. She's helped me out more than I can count."

Vicente's eyes flickered to Rome, then back to Nikki. "Is that right? So you're in the game now, Nikki?"

Nikki swallowed, choosin' her words carefully. "I just do what I gotta do."

Vicente smiled again, but it still didn't feel right. "That's what I like to hear. A woman who knows how to survive. You'll go far with that attitude."

He stepped closer, and Nikki tensed, her guard up. Vicente reached out, his fingers brushin' a strand of hair from her face, his touch cold and possessive. "But you need to be careful, Nikki. This world we live in? It can swallow you if you're not careful."

Nikki held her breath, her body stiff. She didn't like the way he touched her, the way he spoke like he already owned her. But she didn't move. She couldn't. Not with Rome watchin', not with Vicente standin' so close, his presence suffocating.

"Rome," Vicente said, his voice low, his eyes still on Nikki. "You've got yourself a prize. But remember—prizes can be taken."

Rome's expression tightened, but he didn't say anything. Nikki felt the weight of those words settle in her chest. This wasn't just a meetin'. This was a warning.

Vicente stepped back, lettin' the tension ease, but Nikki knew it was only temporary. "Enjoy the rest of your night," he said, his voice casual again. "I'm sure we'll see more of each other soon."

As they left the mansion, Nikki couldn't shake the feelin' that she was walkin' out of a trap she hadn't even realized she was in. Rome was silent, his usual confidence gone, and Nikki didn't dare ask what he was thinkin'.

When they got back in the car, Nikki turned to Rome, her voice sharp. "What the hell was that?"

Rome sighed, his hand tight on the wheel. "Vicente's just testin' you, that's all. He likes you. That's a good thing."

Nikki's stomach churned. "He don't just like me, Rome. He wants somethin'. I don't trust him."

Rome shot her a look, his voice harder now. "You don't have to trust him. You just have to play the game. Vicente runs everything. You want to stay in this life, you better learn how to handle him."

Nikki leaned back, her mind racin'. She was in too deep, and now she was playin' with a man who didn't care about anyone but himself. Rome had gotten her into this, and now she wasn't sure how to get out.

Vicente wasn't like anyone she'd ever met. He was more dangerous, more powerful, and now? He was watchin' her.

And Nikki knew one thing for sure—when men like Vicente watched, they didn't stop until they got what they wanted.

The game had changed. And Nikki was trapped in the middle of it.

Chapter 7: The Trap Tightens

Nikki was never one to get caught slippin'. She played the game too well, moved too smooth through the streets to let anyone lock her down. But since meetin' Vicente, it felt like the walls were closin' in. Everywhere she turned, there he was, like a shadow she couldn't shake.

It started subtle, with the gifts. Expensive. Flashy. Boxes of designer shoes, bags, and jewelry delivered to her door. At first, she figured it was just Vicente tryin' to impress her, flexin' his wealth. But the more she thought about it, the more she realized it wasn't about impressin' her—it was about ownin' her.

The gifts were never asked for, never even discussed. They just appeared. And with them came the unspoken message: *You belong to me now.*

One night, Nikki came home to find a black velvet box sittin' on her bed. Inside was a diamond bracelet, the kind that shimmered under the light like ice. But instead of excitement, she felt a knot form in her stomach. Vicente was makin' his move, and she knew this was just the beginnin'.

Rome, of course, didn't know about the gifts. She kept that part of it quiet, mostly because she didn't know how to explain it. How could she tell him that his boss, his *boss,* was startin' to claim her in ways that went beyond business?

Things escalated when Vicente started callin' her personally, demandin' her presence at private meetin's. They were never about deals, never about business. He wanted her there for *him.* At first, she went because she didn't want to make waves, didn't want to cause any trouble for Rome or herself. But it became clear that these weren't requests. They were orders.

One night, Nikki was loungin' on her couch, scrollin' through her phone, when her screen lit up with a call from an unknown number. Her heart skipped a beat. She knew it was him.

Reluctantly, she answered. "Yeah?"

"Nikki," Vicente's voice came through the line, smooth and calm, but with that undertone of control she had grown to dread. "I'm sendin' a car for you. Be ready in thirty."

She hesitated, grippin' the phone tighter. "I'm kinda busy tonight."

There was a pause on the other end, and when he spoke again, his voice was colder. "I wasn't askin'."

The line went dead, and Nikki felt her chest tighten. This wasn't just some rich dude tryin' to spoil her anymore. This was Vicente puttin' his foot down, showin' her that she didn't have a choice.

Thirty minutes later, a sleek black car pulled up outside her apartment. Nikki sat in the back, her nerves on edge, tryin' to figure out how the hell she had gotten herself into this mess. The car rolled through the city streets, passin' the usual corners where she used to feel in control. Now? Everything felt different. Tense. Darker.

When she arrived at Vicente's mansion, she was led inside, past the usual security guards who barely glanced at her. She was shown into a private room, where Vicente sat behind a massive mahogany desk, his eyes gleamin' with satisfaction as she walked in.

"Nikki," he said, his voice soft but firm. "You look good tonight."

She didn't respond, just stood there, feelin' the weight of his gaze. He motioned for her to sit, and she reluctantly did, knowin' that refusin' wasn't an option.

"I've been thinkin'," Vicente began, his fingers drummin' on the desk. "You and Rome... it's not a good look. You're too valuable to be tied down to someone like him."

Nikki's heart raced, but she kept her face neutral. "Rome and I... we're good. He's takin' care of me."

Vicente's smile faded. "I don't think you understand, Nikki. You belong to me now. Rome? He's not part of this anymore."

She felt the air leave the room. This was it. Vicente wasn't just claimin' her, he was tryin' to cut Rome out completely. And if she resisted? She didn't even want to think about what that might mean.

Vicente leaned forward, his voice low and dangerous. "You keep rollin' with Rome, you put yourself in danger. He's reckless. You? You're smart. You know what's good for you. I can give you everything, Nikki. All you gotta do is play your part."

Nikki's mind raced. She was trapped, and she knew it. If she stayed with Rome, she'd be goin' against Vicente, and that was a death sentence. But leavin' Rome meant turnin' her back on the one person who had helped her rise in this game.

Vicente smiled, seein' her struggle. "Think about it. But don't take too long. You're either with me, or you're against me."

Later that night, Nikki sat on her bed, her head in her hands. She felt like the walls were closin' in, like no matter what move she made, it would be the wrong one. She couldn't shake the feelin' of Vicente's eyes on her, the way he had spoken to her like she was a pawn in his game.

Desperate, she grabbed her phone and called Keisha. She needed someone to talk to, someone who understood the streets but wasn't caught up in the mess she was in.

"Yo, Keish," Nikki said, her voice low. "You got a minute?"

Keisha sounded surprised. "Yeah, girl, what's up? I ain't heard from you in a minute. You good?"

Nikki paused, unsure how to even begin. "It's Vicente. He's... he's pushin' me hard, Keish. He wants me to drop Rome, and I don't know what to do."

There was a silence on the other end, and then Keisha spoke, her voice filled with concern. "Nikki, you need to be careful. Vicente ain't playin'. Once he's got his eyes on you, he ain't lettin' go."

Nikki sighed, her heart heavy. "I feel trapped, Keish. Like no matter what I do, I'm screwed."

"You are," Keisha said bluntly. "But you gotta play this smart. Vicente's dangerous, but so is Rome. You caught between two snakes, girl. One wrong move, and either one of 'em could snap."

Nikki felt a chill run down her spine. She had always thought she could handle herself, that she could play the game without gettin' too deep. But now? She was in over her head, and there was no easy way out.

"What do I do, Keish?" Nikki asked, her voice barely a whisper.

Keisha was silent for a moment, and when she finally spoke, her voice was grim. "You need to keep your head down. Don't piss Vicente off, but don't let him think you're weak either. And whatever you do, don't trust nobody. Not Rome, not Vicente. Nobody."

Nikki nodded, though Keisha couldn't see her. "I hear you."

After they hung up, Nikki stared at the diamond bracelet Vicente had sent her earlier, her stomach churnin'. The more she looked at it, the more it felt like a chain, tightenin' around her wrist, pullin' her deeper into a world she didn't want to be in.

She was trapped. And the worst part? There was no one to save her. Not Rome. Not Keisha. No one.

The trap was tightenin', and Nikki was runnin' out of moves.

Chapter 8: Baby Mama Drama

The sun was barely settin' when Nikki stepped outta the corner store, her mind buzzin' with the weight of everything goin' down between her and Vicente. She was tryin' to figure out her next move, how to balance this delicate situation with Rome, but the second she turned the corner, she spotted trouble headin' her way.

Tasha.

She was walkin' toward Nikki, full of attitude, her face twisted with anger. Nikki had seen her around before, always runnin' her mouth, but she never paid her any mind. Tasha was one of Rome's baby mamas, and from what Nikki knew, she had a temper like fire and a mouth to match.

But today? That fire was burnin' straight at her.

"Yo, Nikki!" Tasha yelled, her voice loud enough to make heads turn on the block. "We need to talk, bitch."

Nikki sighed, already feelin' the heat of this drama comin' her way. She could've kept walkin', could've brushed it off and left Tasha talkin' to herself in the street. But that wasn't Nikki's style. She didn't back down, no matter who it was.

Tasha stomped right up to her, hands on her hips, eyes flarin' with jealousy and rage. She was wearin' too-tight jeans, a crop top showin' off her waist, her weave done up, and her nails longer than they needed to be.

"I know you hearin' me, ho. You think you slick, don't you? You think you can just come in and steal my man like I ain't nobody?"

Nikki raised an eyebrow, lettin' her gaze coolly slide over Tasha. "First of all, I ain't steal nothin'. Rome ain't yours to begin with, Tasha. So whatever you think you know, you better check yourself."

Tasha stepped closer, her voice drippin' with venom. "Bitch, I don't need to check shit! You the one who needs to check yo' place. Rome got a family—he got kids with me! And here you come, actin' like you

"

his woman, like you somebody. But lemme tell you somethin'," Tasha sneered, gettin' all up in Nikki's face, "you ain't shit."

Nikki's jaw tightened, but she kept her composure. "You real bold comin' at me like that. But you need to be mad at *him*, not me. I ain't the one who left you playin' second fiddle."

Tasha's nostrils flared, and before Nikki could react, Tasha shoved her hard in the chest. Nikki stumbled back a step, her blood boilin' now. It was one thing to talk, but puttin' hands on her? That was crossin' a line.

"Oh, you wanna put your hands on me now?" Nikki said, her voice cold and sharp. "I suggest you back the fuck up, Tasha, before this turns into somethin' you can't handle."

Tasha laughed, but it wasn't outta amusement. It was the kind of laugh that sent chills through the air. "You think you tough, huh? You think you runnin' shit 'cause you think you got Rome on a leash? Bitch, I will end you. I'm sick of you thinkin' you got somethin' special. You just the flavor of the month, and when Rome done with you, he comin' back home to me."

Nikki wasn't havin' it anymore. She stepped forward, gettin' all in Tasha's face, her hands clenched into fists. "You real brave talkin' all that shit, but you ain't about to do nothin'. You think you the first chick tryin' to come at me like this? Nah, Tasha. You just another loudmouth, thinkin' she can intimidate me. But I ain't goin' nowhere, so either step off or get knocked the fuck out."

Tasha's face twisted with fury, and before Nikki knew it, she swung. But Nikki was quicker. She ducked, and Tasha's fist sailed through the air, hittin' nothin'. Nikki came up fast, swingin' back, connectin' with Tasha's jaw, sendin' her stumblin' back into a parked car.

The street lit up with noise. People who had been mindin' their business before were suddenly cheerin', their phones out, recordin' the altercation like it was prime-time TV.

Tasha wiped blood from her mouth, her eyes wild with rage. "You gonna regret that, bitch. You don't know who you fuckin' with!"

Nikki stepped forward, standin' her ground. "Try me. I ain't scared of you or whatever drama you tryin' to bring."

Before things could escalate any further, a car screeched up to the curb, and Rome jumped out, lookin' furious. "What the hell is goin' on here?" he yelled, pushin' his way between the two women.

Tasha pointed at Nikki, her voice screamin'. "This bitch! She out here tryin' to act like she got you, like I don't exist!"

Rome held his hands up, tryin' to calm the situation, but it was clear he was caught in the middle. "Tasha, chill. This ain't the place for this shit."

But Tasha wasn't havin' it. "Chill? Oh, so you takin' her side now? I knew it. I fuckin' knew it! You always out here runnin' game on me, and now you got this ho all up in our business? After everything I did for you, Rome?"

Nikki's heart raced as the scene spiraled out of control. She could feel the tension in the air, the buzz from the crowd, the eyes watchin' from every direction. This wasn't just a spat. This was the kinda drama that could blow up her whole spot.

"Rome, handle your baby mama," Nikki said, her voice tight with anger. "I ain't here for this bullshit."

Rome turned to her, his face hard, but Nikki could see the conflict in his eyes. He was stuck between two worlds—Tasha, his past, and Nikki, his present. And no matter what choice he made, somebody was gonna lose.

"Both of y'all need to chill," Rome said, his voice low, tryin' to maintain control. "This ain't the way to handle this. Tasha, you got kids with me, yeah, but that don't mean you can come at Nikki like that. And Nikki... you know I got history with her."

Nikki crossed her arms, feelin' the frustration build. She didn't like bein' caught in the middle of Rome's mess, and Tasha's threats were startin' to get under her skin. But at the same time, she wasn't about to let some jealous baby mama run her off. Rome had made his choice, and Nikki wasn't about to let him forget that.

But Tasha wasn't done. She shoved Rome aside, her eyes locked on Nikki. "You think this over? You think this some petty shit? Nah, bitch. I'm comin' for you, and when I do, you ain't gonna see it comin'. You ain't takin' my man, and you sure as hell ain't takin' my spot."

Nikki took a step forward, her voice calm but filled with ice. "Do what you gotta do, Tasha. But don't make threats you can't back up. You wanna come for me? Then come. But just know, you better bring your A-game."

Rome stepped in again, pushin' them apart. "Enough! Both of y'all need to stop this shit. I ain't dealin' with this no more."

Tasha shot Nikki one last glare before turnin' to Rome. "You better watch your back, Rome. You think this bitch is gonna stick around when shit gets real? Nah. She ain't built for this life."

And with that, she stormed off, leavin' Nikki standin' there, her chest heavin' with adrenaline.

The crowd started to disperse, but the buzz lingered in the air. People were talkin', whisperin', spreadin' the drama like wildfire. Nikki could already hear the gossip echoing through the streets, her name tangled up in Rome's mess.

Rome turned to her, his expression tight. "This ain't good, Nikki. You don't know what you just started."

Nikki squared her shoulders, her eyes cold. "I didn't start shit, Rome. Your baby mama did. Now handle it."

But deep down, Nikki knew this was far from over. Tasha wasn't just talkin'. The streets were buzzin', and when the streets buzzed, it wasn't long before things got real.

Too real.

And Nikki had a feelin' this was only the beginnin' of somethin' much bigger.

Chapter 9: The Setup

The rain came down hard, pelting the windshield of the black Escalade as Nikki sat in the passenger seat, her heart racin'. Her fingers were grippin' the edges of her seat so tight her knuckles turned white. Every instinct in her body told her to jump out and run, but she knew she couldn't. Vicente had her trapped, and the walls were closin' in fast.

This wasn't supposed to be her life. She had always been in control, always the one hustlin' and finessin' her way through the streets. But now? She was caught up in somethin' way bigger than herself, and she couldn't see a way out.

Rome wasn't in the picture right now—he was layin' low after the drama with Tasha. But even if he was around, it wouldn't have mattered. Vicente had taken control of Nikki's life in a way that she never expected. She had been pulled deep into his world, and now there was no more finessin'. It was all about survival.

Vicente had called her earlier that day, givin' her a job. Not a request, not a suggestion. A job. She had to make a drug run for him, somethin' big. Her heart dropped when he laid it all out, but he left no room for argument. She tried to talk her way out of it, but his words were cold, sharp. "You owe me, Nikki. This is how you pay your debt."

And just like that, she was caught. There was no refusin' Vicente. Not if she wanted to stay breathin'.

The Escalade pulled up to an empty warehouse on the edge of the city, the kind of place that looked abandoned but was probably used for all kinds of illegal shit. Nikki's stomach churned as the driver, a stone-faced dude Vicente sent with her, turned off the engine.

"Get out," he grunted, not even lookin' at her.

Nikki swallowed hard, tryin' to steady herself. She was out of her depth here, and the reality of it was hittin' her harder than she expected. She was about to step into a situation that could go bad in a million ways. Cops, rival crews, setups—she didn't know what she was walkin' into, and it terrified her.

But she got out of the car anyway, pullin' her hood over her head as the rain continued to pour. The warehouse loomed ahead, dark and silent except for the flicker of a single streetlight on the corner.

"Let's go," the driver barked, pushin' her toward the door.

Nikki's heart was poundin' in her chest as they stepped inside the warehouse. The air was thick with the smell of mold and damp concrete, the kind of place where bad shit happened and nobody ever asked questions. Inside, a couple of men stood near a table, surrounded by bricks of cocaine and duffle bags stuffed with cash.

The scene felt surreal, like somethin' out of a movie. But this was real. Too real.

"Where's Vicente's money?" one of the men asked, his voice rough as he eyed Nikki.

She nodded toward the duffle bag she was carryin', her hands shakin' just enough for him to notice. The man smirked, shakin' his head. "She don't look like she's used to this."

The words cut deep, but Nikki kept her face stone cold. She wasn't about to let them see her sweat, not in this place. "Vicente sent me. You got the product or not?"

The man's smirk faded as he motioned for the other guy to start packin' up the duffle bags. "Yeah, we got it. Just make sure you take it straight back. No detours, no bullshit."

Nikki nodded, but her stomach twisted tighter with every second that passed. She just wanted to grab the bags and get the hell out of there. She could feel the weight of everything pressin' down on her, the stakes higher than anything she'd dealt with before.

But as the deal was goin' down, somethin' shifted in the air. A sudden tension. Nikki's senses went into overdrive as the sound of sirens echoed faintly in the distance.

"Yo, you hear that?" one of the men said, his eyes wide with panic.

"Shit, the cops!" another guy yelled, his voice frantic.

Panic spread like wildfire through the warehouse. Nikki's heart stopped as she realized what was happenin'. This wasn't just a simple drug run—it was a fuckin' setup.

The men scrambled, grabbin' the drugs and tryin' to disappear. But it was too late. The sirens were closin' in, louder now, and blue lights flashed through the warehouse windows. Nikki's mind raced, searchin' for an exit. She couldn't get caught. She wouldn't get caught.

Without thinkin', she grabbed the nearest bag and bolted for the back door. The driver who'd brought her was already gone, disappearin' into the rain like a ghost. Nikki ran as fast as her legs would carry her, duckin' out the back and into the alley. She could hear the sound of doors crashin' open behind her, the cops pourin' into the warehouse, shoutin' orders.

Her breath was comin' in ragged gasps as she sprinted down the narrow street, her feet splashin' through puddles, her hood clingin' to her soaked hair. She didn't stop, didn't look back. Her only thought was gettin' as far away from that place as possible.

By the time she reached a side street, her body was screamin' for air, her lungs burnin'. She collapsed against a wall, tryin' to catch her breath, her heart hammerin' in her chest. She had barely escaped, barely missed gettin' locked up. And the worst part? She knew this was just the beginnin'.

Hours later, Nikki stood in Vicente's office, her clothes still wet from the rain, her body tremblin' with a mix of fear and adrenaline. Vicente sat behind his desk, his face calm and unreadable, like the chaos she had just survived didn't mean shit to him.

"You set me up," Nikki hissed, her voice raw with anger.

Vicente leaned back in his chair, his fingers steepled under his chin. "Set you up? No, Nikki. I gave you a test. You passed."

Nikki's hands clenched into fists. "I almost got fuckin' locked up, Vicente! The cops were all over that place. If I hadn't run, I'd be in a cell right now."

Vicente's eyes narrowed, his voice cold and sharp. "But you didn't get caught. And that's what matters."

Nikki's breath caught in her throat. He wasn't listenin'. He didn't care. To him, she was just another pawn in his game, and the fact that she had barely escaped meant nothin' to him. He was testin' her, pushin' her limits, seein' how far he could control her.

"You own me now, don't you?" Nikki said, her voice barely a whisper, but the weight of her words hung heavy in the room.

Vicente smiled, slow and sinister. "You're smarter than I thought. Yes, Nikki. I own you now. And as long as you keep doin' what I say, you'll stay alive. But if you cross me?" He leaned forward, his eyes dark with menace. "Then it's over. Understand?"

Nikki's heart sank as the reality of her situation hit her like a brick. She had lost control of her life. Vicente had her locked in, and there was no escape. Not from him, not from the streets.

The walls were closin' in, and Nikki was trapped.

She nodded, her throat tight, her mind numb. "I understand."

Vicente leaned back, satisfied. "Good. Now, get some rest. We've got more work to do."

As she walked out of his office, her hands still shakin', Nikki knew one thing for sure—she had to find a way out. Before the streets swallowed her whole.

But the more she thought about it, the more she realized... there might not be a way out.

Chapter 10: Heartbreak and Deception

Nikki sat on the edge of her bed, starin' out the window as the rain beat down, matching the storm inside her head. The events of the past few days weighed heavy on her chest, each moment replaying over and over like a bad dream she couldn't wake up from. She couldn't believe how far things had spiraled.

Everything had gone to shit.

Her phone buzzed beside her, pullin' her out of her thoughts. She glanced down and saw the message light up: Rome: "We need to talk."

She felt her stomach twist. Just readin' his name now sent a wave of disgust through her. The man she thought she could trust, the one who had pulled her into this game, had played her. She had heard whispers—low-key rumors from the streets, but she didn't want to believe it. Rome, the one person who was supposed to be ridin' for her, was the same man who'd handed her over to Vicente like a pawn.

Nikki stood up, grabbin' her jacket. She needed answers, and she wasn't about to wait for Rome to make his move. This time, she was comin' for him.

Rome's spot was a sleek penthouse downtown, the kind of place that flaunted his money and connections. Nikki had spent more than a few nights there, wrapped up in the luxury, thinkin' she was the one who had won the prize. But now? Now the place felt like a damn lie. A façade for the bullshit Rome had been feedin' her.

She stormed through the lobby and straight up to the top floor, not even givin' the security a chance to stop her. Her heart was poundin', and her mind was on fire. She didn't know what she was gonna do when she saw him, but one thing was clear—Rome was about to get the reckoning he deserved.

When she reached the door, she didn't knock. She pounded, her fist slammin' against the wood, her blood boilin'. "Rome! Open the fuckin' door!"

The door swung open a moment later, and there he was—Rome, standin' in the doorway, lookin' too calm for what was about to go down. He was dressed in his usual designer gear, gold chains glintin' against his chest, like he had no worries in the world.

"What the hell you bangin' my door for?" he asked, his voice cool, almost amused.

Nikki pushed past him, stormin' into the penthouse. "We need to talk."

Rome closed the door behind her, his expression still unreadable. "Oh, we talkin' now? Aight, then. Let's hear it."

Nikki spun around, her eyes blazin'. "I know what you did, Rome. I know you set me up with Vicente."

For a moment, there was silence. Rome's face didn't even flinch. He just stared at her, like she was talkin' about the weather, not about the fact that he had betrayed her.

"You knew Vicente would trap me in this bullshit," Nikki continued, her voice tremblin' with anger. "You used me. From the jump, you was playin' me like all the other marks."

Rome's lips curled into a cold smirk. "And? What you thought this was, Nikki? A love story? Nah, you know what this is. This is the streets. Everybody playin' a role, and you just happen to be playin' yours."

Nikki's chest tightened. "So I was just a fuckin' pawn to you?"

Rome's eyes darkened, his voice turnin' hard. "You been playin' the game long enough to know how it works, Nikki. You think you wasn't playin' me too? You been finessin' dudes for years, and now you mad 'cause somebody finally got one over on you? You wanted the money, the power, the trips—well, this is what comes with it."

Nikki felt like the air was bein' ripped outta her lungs. She had been played before, sure, but never like this. Not by someone she thought had her back.

"All that shit you told me," she said, her voice low, shaky. "About us, about you and me buildin' somethin'? It was all a fuckin' lie?"

Rome didn't even blink. "I told you what I needed to tell you. You fell for it. You played yourself."

Nikki's vision blurred with anger. Her hand shot out before she could stop herself, slappin' him across the face with everything she had. The sound echoed through the room, but Rome didn't flinch. He just looked at her, his expression cold and hard as stone.

"You done?" he asked, his voice so calm it made her skin crawl.

Tears burned at the back of Nikki's eyes, but she refused to let them fall. She wasn't about to give him the satisfaction of seein' her break. "Fuck you, Rome. I gave up everything for you."

Rome shook his head. "You gave up nothin'. You just thought you could be somethin' more. But I had plans, Nikki. You was just a piece in the game."

Nikki's fists clenched at her sides, her whole body tremblin' with rage. She had trusted him. She had fallen for his lies, let herself get caught up in the fantasy he sold her, and now it felt like her whole world was crumblin'.

"You sold me out to Vicente," she said through gritted teeth. "You knew what he was about to do, and you didn't even give a fuck."

Rome shrugged, like it wasn't a big deal. "Vicente wanted you. I made sure it worked out. That's business, Nikki. You think he'd let you walk away without payin' your dues? You should be thankin' me. I made sure you stayed in the game."

"In the game?" Nikki spat, her voice filled with venom. "I'm trapped, Rome! He fuckin' owns me now. I can't move without him pullin' the strings, and you let that happen."

Rome finally dropped the smirk, his voice turnin' sharp. "You think you had a choice? You think I had a choice? This ain't some fairy tale, Nikki. You either play by the rules or get taken out. Vicente don't take kindly to people steppin' outta line, and neither should you."

Nikki's heart pounded in her chest. She had never felt this level of betrayal before, not even from the men she used to con. Rome wasn't just another dude—he was supposed to be her partner, the one who had her back in this messed-up world. And now she realized he was just another liar, another snake in the streets.

"I trusted you," she said, her voice barely above a whisper.

Rome stepped closer, his eyes lockin' on hers. "That's your problem, Nikki. You trust too much. You forget who you are and where you from. Ain't nobody out here lookin' out for you. Not me, not Vicente, not nobody. The streets don't owe you shit."

Nikki felt the weight of his words crash down on her. Everything she had built, everything she thought she had, was crumblin' beneath her feet. The money, the power, the connections—it was all built on lies. And now she was left with nothin' but the cold reality of her situation.

Rome turned away, grabbin' his keys from the counter. "You wanna be mad? Be mad at yourself. You played the game, and you lost. That's life."

Nikki stood there, frozen, her mind racin'. She had been betrayed, used, and thrown aside like she didn't matter. But deep down, she knew one thing—she wasn't about to let this be the end. She had been knocked down before, but she always got back up. And now? Now she was gonna take back control of her life.

Even if it killed her.

As Rome walked toward the door, Nikki's voice cut through the silence. "You think you won, but you haven't seen the last of me. I ain't no pawn, and I sure as hell ain't yours anymore."

Rome glanced back, his eyes cold and dismissive. "Do what you gotta do, Nikki. But remember—you ain't runnin' shit."

The door slammed shut behind him, leavin' Nikki standin' alone in the empty penthouse, her chest heavy with betrayal, anger, and heartbreak. But in that moment, she made a promise to herself.

She would find a way out of this mess. She would take back what was hers.

And when she did?

Rome and Vicente would both regret the day they ever crossed her.

Chapter 11: The Plan

The streets were watchin'. Nikki knew it. Every move she made felt like someone had eyes on her, waitin' for her to trip up. She was playin' a dangerous game, one where the stakes weren't just money or status. It was her life on the line, and every step had to be calculated, precise. One wrong move and Vicente would have her buried under the concrete before anyone knew she was missin'.

But Nikki wasn't about to let herself go out like that. She wasn't some pawn to be tossed aside. If Vicente thought he owned her, he was wrong. She had to find a way out, a way to take control of her life again. And that meant goin' back to what she knew best—runnin' the game.

She needed money. Fast. Enough to disappear, to slip out of Vicente's clutches before he realized what was goin' down. And she had just the man in mind.

His name was Bradley. A rich businessman she had conned a couple years back when she was still finessin' fools for cash and gifts. He was one of the big fish she'd reeled in, the kind that spent without thinkin' twice and believed every sweet word she whispered in his ear. Nikki had let him think he had won her over, but when she'd drained his bank account dry, she vanished like a ghost.

Now, she needed to bring him back into her web.

Nikki sat in front of her cracked mirror, applyin' her makeup with careful precision. She knew how to play the part—soft, seductive, innocent enough to make them think they had control. Bradley was easy to read, and she was ready to make him believe whatever story she had to sell.

As she finished gettin' ready, she stared at herself in the mirror, her mind racin'. This was risky—every second she spent tryin' to run this hustle was a second closer to Vicente findin' out. And if he knew she was tryin' to skip out on him, he'd come down on her like a storm. But Nikki didn't have a choice. She was done bein' somebody else's puppet.

She met Bradley at an upscale bar in the city, the kind of place where the lights were low and the drinks were expensive. He looked the same as she remembered—clean-cut, wearin' a suit that probably cost more than most people's rent. His face lit up when he saw her, and Nikki knew she had him right where she wanted.

"Nikki, damn, it's been a minute," Bradley said as he stood up, offerin' her a smooth smile. "You look as beautiful as ever."

Nikki smiled back, lettin' her lips curl just enough to keep him hooked. "It's been too long, Bradley. I'm sorry for disappearin' like that. Life got... complicated."

He raised an eyebrow, but the curiosity in his eyes told her he wasn't mad—he was intrigued. "Complicated, huh? You back now?"

"For now," Nikki replied, her voice soft, vulnerable. "But I could really use someone like you in my life again, Bradley. Someone who understands me."

Bradley's eyes gleamed as he motioned for her to sit down. "You know I always had a soft spot for you, Nikki. What's goin' on?"

Nikki hesitated for just a second, calculatin' her words carefully. "I need help. I got involved with the wrong people. I thought I could handle it, but it's too much now. I need to get out."

Bradley leaned in, his voice low. "What kind of trouble we talkin' about?"

Nikki sighed, lowerin' her eyes just enough to play the part. "I can't say too much. Just... it's bad. And if I don't disappear soon, I'm done for."

Bradley's hand reached across the table, touchin' hers. "You know I got you, Nikki. Whatever you need."

Her heart raced as she felt the words leave his mouth. That was exactly what she wanted to hear. But deep down, she knew it wasn't gonna be that easy. Bradley was a mark, yeah, but Vicente was watchin'. He always was.

"I need money, Brad. A lot of it. I wouldn't ask if it wasn't life or death."

He hesitated, glancin' around the room, as if weighin' the risk in his head. But Nikki saw it in his eyes—he was already sold. The thrill of savin' her, the chance to be her knight in shinin' armor, it was too much for a man like him to resist.

"How much we talkin'?"

Nikki took a deep breath. "I need at least fifty grand. Enough to cover my tracks and get out of the city without anyone followin' me."

Bradley blinked, clearly not expectin' that number. But after a moment, he nodded. "I can do that. It might take me a couple days to pull it together, but I'll make it happen."

Nikki smiled, leanin' in closer, lettin' her hand rest on his arm. "Thank you, Bradley. You don't know what this means to me."

He grinned, clearly feelin' like the hero. "Anything for you, Nikki. I'm just glad I can help."

As Nikki walked out of the bar, her heels clickin' against the pavement, her mind raced with a mix of relief and anxiety. She had pulled it off. Bradley was in, and the money was gonna come through. But the closer she got to her freedom, the more she felt the weight of Vicente's presence.

Every shadow, every passing car, felt like a threat. She knew he had eyes everywhere. And if he found out she was tryin' to run, she wouldn't make it out of the city alive.

The next day, she met up with Keisha at their usual spot—a run-down diner off the main strip, where nobody paid attention to the conversations happenin' in the back booths. Keisha was the only one she could trust now, the only one who understood the game they were both caught up in.

"So what's the plan?" Keisha asked, her eyes narrowin' as she sipped her coffee. "You really think Bradley's gonna come through?"

Nikki nodded, though there was doubt creepin' in. "Yeah, he will. But I gotta move fast. Vicente's gettin' suspicious."

Keisha shook her head. "You playin' a dangerous game, girl. Vicente don't let nobody just walk away."

Nikki sighed, leanin' back in her seat. "I know. But I ain't got a choice. It's this or I end up dead. I'm done bein' his puppet."

Keisha looked at her for a long moment before speakin'. "You sure you got this, Nikki? Once you make that move, there's no goin' back."

Nikki stared out the window, watchin' the streets buzz with life. She knew what was at stake. She knew the risks. But she also knew that if she didn't try, she'd be stuck under Vicente's thumb forever.

"I got no other option, Keish. I gotta do this."

Keisha nodded slowly, her expression serious. "Aight. Just be careful. I don't want to hear about you endin' up in a ditch somewhere."

Nikki forced a smile, though the fear gnawed at her insides. "I won't. I'm gonna pull this off."

But even as the words left her mouth, she felt the weight of the truth settlin' in. The game was dangerous, and she was playin' with fire. One wrong move, and Vicente would burn her to ashes.

She had a few days to pull everything together. A few days to get the money, disappear, and finally break free.

But as she walked back to her apartment that night, a chill crept down her spine. She could feel it in the air—someone was watchin'. The streets were whisperin', and Nikki knew Vicente wasn't far behind.

Time was runnin' out.

And the question that lingered in her mind was simple:

Could she make it out before it was too late?

Chapter 12: The Downfall Begins

The streets had a way of talkin'. No matter how slick you moved, no matter how tight you kept your circle, people always knew somethin'. And right now, Nikki could feel the streets buzzin' with her name. Eyes she couldn't see were followin' her every move. Vicente was gettin' suspicious, and she knew it. The walls were closin' in.

Everywhere she went, it felt like somebody was watchin'. The hood was full of whispers—low voices, side glances, heads turnin' just as she passed by. Nikki kept her head high, but inside, she was unravelin'. She knew how the game worked, and she could feel the noose gettin' tighter around her neck with each day that passed. Vicente wasn't the type to let things slide, and she had been movin' too fast, makin' plans behind his back.

Her phone buzzed in her pocket, snappin' her back to reality. She pulled it out, her stomach churnin' when she saw the name on the screen. **Vicente.**

She hesitated, feelin' that cold sweat drip down her spine. He never called outta nowhere. Not unless somethin' was up.

With shaky hands, she answered. "Yeah?"

"Nikki," Vicente's voice was smooth, but she could hear the edge underneath, like a knife waitin' to slice. "You been keepin' busy lately. Lotta movement from your side."

Her throat tightened. "Just handlin' business, Vicente. You know how it is."

There was a pause, then a low chuckle on the other end. "Yeah, I know how it is. But you movin' like you tryin' to disappear on me. You know I don't like surprises."

Nikki's heart raced, her mind spinnin'. He knew somethin'. He had to. "Nah, ain't nothin' like that. I'm just... tryna make sure everything stays smooth."

"Good," Vicente replied, his voice colder now. "Because I don't like when people start actin' outta pocket. You gettin' what I'm sayin', right?"

She swallowed hard, her pulse poundin' in her ears. "I hear you, Vicente."

"Don't make me have to remind you what happens when people forget their place."

The line went dead, leavin' Nikki standin' there, her stomach twisted into knots. She shoved the phone back into her pocket, tryin' to keep her cool, but she couldn't shake the feelin' that Vicente was already ten steps ahead of her.

She had to move fast.

That night, Nikki headed to one of her usual spots, a lowkey bar on the edge of town where nobody asked questions. It was the kind of place where deals went down in the back, and cops didn't bother stoppin' by unless they had a reason. She needed a drink, somethin' to steady her nerves, but more than that, she needed to figure out what her next move was.

As soon as she walked in, she could feel the eyes on her. Familiar faces turned to watch her pass, but there was somethin' different in the air tonight. More than just curiosity. There was suspicion.

Keisha was already there, sittin' in their usual booth in the back, lookin' tense. Nikki slid into the seat across from her, and before she could even say a word, Keisha leaned forward, her voice low and urgent.

"Yo, you hearin' what they sayin' in the streets?"

Nikki nodded, her chest tight. "I feel it, Keish. It's like everybody's waitin' for somethin' to pop off."

Keisha's eyes darted around the bar before lockin' back on Nikki. "Vicente's plottin'. Word is, he knows somebody in his crew's movin' funny, and he's about to make a real example outta them."

Nikki's stomach dropped. She didn't need to ask who that somebody was. She could feel Vicente's grip on her, squeezin' tighter by the minute.

"You think he knows?" Nikki whispered, her voice barely audible over the music.

Keisha looked at her, dead serious. "If he don't know yet, he's damn close. You gotta be careful. You tryin' to run, he'll know."

Nikki sighed, feelin' trapped. She had thought she could play this game smarter than anyone else, but now the pieces were fallin' apart in her hands. "I don't got much of a choice. If I stay, I'm as good as dead."

Keisha nodded slowly, her face grim. "I know. But you better be ready to move when shit goes down. And trust me, Nikki... it's goin' down soon."

Days passed, and with each one, Nikki felt the noose tighten. She could see Vicente's men more often now, lurkin' in the background like shadows. They never said a word, but their presence was heavy, suffocatin'. Every time she left her apartment, they were there. Every time she made a call or met with someone, she knew it was bein' watched.

The paranoia was settin' in. Hard.

One afternoon, Nikki was walkin' down the block, her mind racin', when she caught sight of a black SUV parked across the street. She recognized it immediately—one of Vicente's cars. Her heart skipped a beat, but she kept walkin', actin' like she hadn't noticed.

As she turned the corner, she glanced over her shoulder, and sure enough, the SUV was followin'. Her pulse quickened. She needed to move fast. She ducked into an alley, quickenin' her pace, her hands clammy with fear.

She didn't know how much time she had left before Vicente made his move, but she knew it wasn't much.

That night, Nikki lay in bed, starin' at the ceiling, her mind runnin' through every scenario. Bradley had promised to come through with the money, but it was takin' too long. If she didn't have the cash to disappear soon, Vicente would close in, and she'd be left with nothin' but her regrets.

Her phone buzzed on the nightstand, and she grabbed it, hopin' it was Bradley with good news. But instead, her heart sank as she read the message:

Bradley: "Somethin's come up. Gonna need a little more time to get the money together. Hang tight."

"Fuck," Nikki muttered, throwin' her phone down on the bed. She didn't have time. Every minute that passed felt like a countdown to her death. The streets were talkin', and Vicente was listenin'.

Her options were runnin' out.

The next day, Nikki met with Keisha again, the tension between them thick. Nikki was losin' control, and they both knew it. She was caught in a game where the rules kept changin', and she was always a step behind.

"You gotta get that money soon, Nikki," Keisha said, her voice low but firm. "Vicente ain't playin'. You hear what he did to that dude last week?"

Nikki shook her head, dread twistin' in her gut. "What happened?"

Keisha leaned in, her voice barely a whisper. "Dude thought he could run game on Vicente, tryin' to skim off the top. Vicente found out, had him tied up in an abandoned warehouse. Let his men take turns beatin' him 'til he was barely breathin'. Then... they dumped him in the river."

Nikki's blood ran cold. She could see it playin' out in her mind, the violence, the brutality. Vicente didn't just make examples—he destroyed people. And if she wasn't careful, she'd be next.

"I gotta get out," Nikki muttered, her eyes dartin' around like she was expectin' Vicente's men to pop outta nowhere.

Keisha reached across the table, grabbin' Nikki's hand. "I know, girl. But you gotta be smart. Don't let him see you sweatin'. If he thinks you're scared, he'll move faster."

Nikki nodded, but her mind was racin'. She was runnin' outta time, and she knew it. The streets were closin' in, and the game was almost up.

She stood up, her chest tight with fear. "I'm gonna make this right, Keish. I have to."

Keisha looked up at her, concern flashin' in her eyes. "Just be careful. He's watchin' you."

Nikki turned and walked out into the night, the weight of the world on her shoulders. She could feel it—the noose was tightenin', and soon, Vicente would make his move.

The question was: would Nikki be ready, or was it already too late?

Chapter 13: A Bloody Betrayal

The streets were cold that night. A chill ran through the air, slicing right through Nikki's jacket as she stood outside the rundown hotel, waiting for her mark to show up. She had one last hustle to pull before she could disappear. Bradley's money still hadn't come through, and her escape plan was falling apart. But she had another move. There was always another move.

She hadn't told Keisha about this one. Somethin' in her gut told her to keep quiet, even though she always confided in her best friend. She couldn't explain it, but after everything that had gone down, Nikki felt like the walls were closin' in, and she didn't trust anybody. Not anymore. She was playin' the game on her own now.

As she paced back and forth, tryin' to calm her nerves, her phone buzzed. She pulled it out, hopin' it was her mark tellin' her he was close. Instead, it was Keisha.

Keisha: *"Yo, where you at?"*

Nikki hesitated before typing a quick lie.

Nikki: *"Just handlin' some business. What's up?"*

Keisha: *"I need to see you. It's urgent."*

Nikki frowned. Keisha was rarely urgent about anything, especially since things had been tense between them lately. She typed back.

Nikki: *"Can't right now. I'll hit you later."*

She slid her phone back into her pocket, tryin' to shake the uneasy feelin' creepin' up her spine. She didn't have time to deal with whatever Keisha needed right now. Not with her whole escape dependin' on this last con.

Her mark was a rich executive from out of town, the kind who never asked too many questions and never saw the setup comin'. Nikki had it all planned—get him into a hotel room, make him feel special, then rob him blind. Easy. She just needed the cash and a way out.

But deep down, she couldn't ignore the feelin' that somethin' was off.

As she stood there, her mind racing, she heard footsteps behind her. Nikki tensed, turnin' around quickly, but before she could react, a black SUV screeched to a stop in front of her. Her heart dropped into her stomach.

Vicente's men.

Two of them jumped out, their eyes locked on her with deadly intent. Nikki's breath caught in her throat as she took a step back, her mind goin' into overdrive. Why were they on her like this? She hadn't told anyone about any plans.

Except...

Keisha.

The realization hit her like a punch to the gut. Keisha had betrayed her. Her only friend, the one person she thought she could trust, had sold her out.

"Yo, you ain't goin' nowhere, Nikki," one of the men growled as they closed in on her. His hand rested on the gun at his waist, his eyes cold and predatory. "Vicente don't like when people try to run."

Nikki's heart pounded in her chest, and her instincts screamed at her to move. She didn't wait for them to get any closer. She bolted.

Her feet slammed against the pavement as she sprinted down the street, her breath comin' in ragged gasps. The sound of footsteps echoed behind her—Vicente's men were fast, but Nikki was faster. Years of hustlin' had taught her how to run, how to slip away when shit hit the fan.

But this was different. This wasn't some angry mark or a low-level thug. These were Vicente's men, and they wouldn't stop until they had her.

She cut through an alley, the darkness swallowing her whole, but she could hear the SUV screechin' around the corner, tryin' to follow.

Sweat dripped down her forehead as she darted between dumpsters and broken glass, her mind screamin' for a way out.

But she was runnin' out of time. And options.

As she rounded another corner, she tripped, her foot catchin' on a piece of debris. Nikki hit the ground hard, her palms scrapin' against the concrete, blood oozin' from her skin. She cursed under her breath, pushin' herself up just as one of Vicente's men came into view at the end of the alley.

"Got you now, bitch," he sneered, pullin' his gun from his waistband.

Nikki's heart stopped for a split second as she stared down the barrel of the gun, her body frozen in fear. But then, adrenaline kicked in, and she dove to the side just as he pulled the trigger. The gunshot echoed through the alley, the bullet ricocheting off the wall, missin' her by inches.

She scrambled to her feet, her body screamin' in pain, and took off again. Her mind raced. She had to get outta this. She couldn't let them catch her. Not like this.

The sounds of the SUV grew closer, the headlights sweepin' through the alley as they tried to corner her. Nikki pushed herself harder, her breath ragged and desperate. She spotted an open door at the end of the alley and made a beeline for it.

She burst through the door, slamming it shut behind her, and found herself in an old, abandoned warehouse. The air was thick with dust and the smell of rusted metal. Nikki leaned against the door, tryin' to catch her breath, her heart poundin' so loud she could barely hear anything else.

She knew she didn't have much time. Vicente's men wouldn't give up that easy.

Her mind raced, tryin' to piece together what had just happened. Keisha. She had sold her out. For what? Money? Fear of Vicente? Nikki felt a stab of pain deep in her chest, not just from the betrayal, but from the realization that she was truly alone now.

There was nobody left to trust.

She heard footsteps outside the door, and her body tensed. They were comin'. Nikki's mind spun with panic, but she forced herself to focus. She needed a way out. Somethin'. Anything.

She spotted a fire escape ladder on the far wall and sprinted toward it. Just as she reached the ladder, the door crashed open behind her, and Vicente's men stormed in, their guns drawn.

"There she is!" one of them yelled, his eyes wild with adrenaline.

Nikki didn't waste a second. She grabbed the ladder and hauled herself up, her muscles burnin' with every step. The men below fired their guns, bullets flyin' past her, ricocheting off the metal steps, but she kept climbin', desperate to get away.

When she reached the roof, she pulled herself up and ran to the edge, lookin' for a way down. The city stretched out beneath her, the lights of the streets blurin' together in the distance. She could hear the men climbin' the ladder behind her, their voices filled with rage.

Nikki's chest heaved as she looked down at the alley below. The drop was steep, but there was a fire escape on the next building over. If she could just make it across...

She didn't think. She just moved.

With a burst of adrenaline, Nikki sprinted to the edge of the roof and jumped. Her body soared through the air, her heart poundin' in her throat. For a split second, she thought she wouldn't make it. But her hands caught the edge of the fire escape, and she clung to it, her arms screamin' in pain.

She pulled herself up, her body achin', and scrambled down the fire escape, her breath comin' in shallow gasps. Behind her, she could hear Vicente's men shoutin', their footsteps echoing on the roof. But they were too slow. She was already halfway down the building by the time they reached the edge.

Nikki hit the ground hard, her legs bucklin' beneath her, but she didn't stop. She pushed herself up and took off runnin', her mind focused on one thing: survival.

As she ran through the dark streets, the sounds of the city drownin' out the chaos behind her, Nikki knew one thing for sure.

She couldn't trust nobody.

Not even the people she thought had her back.

And now? She was on her own.

Chapter 14: Cornered

Nikki's lungs burned, her legs were achin', and her heart pounded in her chest like a drum as she darted through the back alleys of the city. The sound of footsteps echoed behind her, Vicente's men closin' in, their voices carryin' through the damp night air. She couldn't stop. Not now. Not ever. If they caught her, it was over.

She'd been on the run for hours, maybe longer. Time didn't mean nothin' when you were runnin' for your life. She had lost track of the streets she'd passed, the corners she'd cut, tryin' to shake the eyes that always seemed to be on her.

Her body screamed for a break, for a moment to catch her breath, but there was no time for that. Everywhere she went, someone recognized her. The streets were talkin'. She could hear her name whispered in the shadows, people pointin', watchin'. They knew who she was, and they knew what was comin'.

Nikki stumbled into another alley, her legs heavy with exhaustion, and collapsed against a brick wall. She could hear the distant roar of a car engine, probably one of Vicente's blacked-out SUVs, prowlin' the streets like a predator lookin' for prey. They weren't far behind.

Her mind raced, tryin' to find a way out. There had to be somewhere she could go, someone who could help. But every option she thought of felt like a dead end. She had burned too many bridges. Keisha had sold her out, and now she couldn't even trust her own shadow.

She fumbled for her phone, her hands shakin'. There was one person she hadn't reached out to yet. One person who, despite everything, might still have some kind of loyalty to her.

Rome.

She hesitated, her thumb hoverin' over his number. The last time they had spoken, he made it clear she was just another pawn in his game. But she had no choice. She needed help, and fast. She dialed his number, prayin' he'd pick up.

The phone rang, echoing in the quiet alley, each ring feelin' like a death sentence. Nikki held her breath, her body frozen with anticipation. Then, finally, the call connected.

"What you want?" Rome's voice was cold, detached. No trace of the man she thought she knew.

"Rome, I need you," Nikki gasped, her voice barely steady. "Vicente's men are after me. They're closin' in. I need somewhere to hide."

There was a long pause, the silence stretchin' between them like a chasm. Nikki could feel her heart sinkin', her hope slippin' away.

"Nah, Nikki," Rome finally said, his voice low and ruthless. "You made your bed. Now you gon' have to lay in it."

Nikki's chest tightened, her stomach churnin' with fear and betrayal. "Rome, please. You don't understand. If they catch me, I'm dead."

Rome let out a cold laugh, the sound cuttin' through her like a blade. "I don't give a damn. You just another liability now. You ain't my problem no more."

The line went dead.

Nikki stared at the screen, disbelief floodin' her system. Rome had really left her out to dry. After everything they'd been through, after all the ways she had helped him rise in the game, he had just turned his back on her.

She threw the phone against the wall, watchin' it shatter into pieces. Tears welled up in her eyes, but she swallowed them back. There was no time for breakin' down. She had to move. Fast.

The streets were growin' darker, and every corner felt like a trap. Nikki kept her head low, movin' through the city like a ghost, tryin' to stay invisible. But it was gettin' harder. Too many people knew her face now. Too many people had seen her with Vicente, and they knew she wasn't just some random chick.

As she turned another corner, she spotted a group of men hangin' by a bodega. They looked rough—tattoos on their faces, eyes cold and hard. One of them caught her eye, his gaze lockin' on her like a predator.

"Nikki, right?" he called out, his voice filled with malice.

Nikki didn't answer. She kept walkin', quickenin' her pace, but she could feel them movin' toward her.

"You ain't gon' get far," the man taunted, his voice echoing in the empty street. "Vicente got a price on your head. You think you can outrun that?"

Her blood ran cold. She picked up speed, her legs movin' faster, even though her muscles were screamin' for rest. She could hear the men laughin' behind her, but they didn't follow. They didn't have to. They knew the game, and they knew she wouldn't make it out. Not with Vicente's men breathin' down her neck.

She ducked into another alley, her mind racin', her breath comin' in ragged gasps. Her whole body was tremblin', and she could feel the panic settin' in. She was cornered, and there was no way out.

Nikki leaned against the wall, tryin' to gather her thoughts, tryin' to figure out her next move. But it was hard to think straight when every breath felt like it could be her last.

Suddenly, she heard the screech of tires at the end of the alley. A black SUV pulled up, its headlights blazin' like searchlights in the darkness. The doors swung open, and two men stepped out, their faces hidden by the shadows, but Nikki knew who they were.

Vicente's men. They had found her.

Her heart pounded in her chest as she backed away, her eyes searchin' for an exit. But there was nowhere to go. She was trapped.

"End of the line, Nikki," one of the men said, his voice cold and hard. "Vicente wants you alive, but if you keep runnin', we can change that real quick."

Nikki's mind raced. She knew Vicente didn't want her dead—at least not yet. He wanted to make an example out of her, to show the streets what happened when you crossed him. But these men? They weren't as patient.

She had seconds to decide. Fight or flight.

Without thinkin', Nikki bolted toward the opposite end of the alley, her feet slappin' against the pavement as she ran for her life. The men shouted, their footsteps poundin' behind her as they gave chase.

The alley was narrow, with garbage bags piled high and debris scatterin' the ground. Nikki stumbled, nearly losin' her balance, but she pushed herself harder, her heart slammin' in her chest. She could hear the men closin' in, their voices growin' louder, more aggressive.

She reached the end of the alley and skidded to a stop, her eyes widenin' in terror. There was a brick wall in front of her—too high to climb, too solid to break through. She was trapped.

"Nowhere left to go, Nikki," one of the men sneered as they approached, their guns drawn. "Time to face the music."

Nikki's breath came in short, panicked bursts as she backed against the wall. Her mind spun, lookin' for any way out, any chance at survival. But there was nothin'.

The men stepped closer, their eyes glintin' with cruel satisfaction. They knew they had her.

"Vicente's gonna be real happy to see you," one of them said, smirkin'. "But first, we're gonna make sure you remember why you don't cross him."

As they closed in, Nikki's body tensed, her mind screamin' for a miracle. She had come so far, survived so much, but now? Now she was cornered, with nowhere left to run.

And as the darkness of the alley swallowed her whole, she knew one thing for certain:

Her time was runnin' out.

Chapter 15: The Escape Plan

Nikki sat in the shadows of a dingy, run-down motel room, the flickering light from the cracked window barely enough to see her own reflection in the mirror. Her body was trembling, but it wasn't from fear—it was the weight of desperation bearing down on her. Every second felt like a ticking bomb, ready to blow at any moment. The streets were alive with whispers, and her name was at the center of all of them.

Vicente's men were out there, scouring every corner, every dark alley, lookin' for her. She had managed to slip away after that last chase, but she knew she wasn't safe. Not for long. The city was too small, the people too nosy. And with the Carnival comin' up, the whole island was about to turn into a crowded, chaotic mess.

That was her chance. The Carnival was the only cover big enough to hide her movements, the perfect distraction while she slipped out of the Caribbean for good. But first, she needed a passport. A clean one. And that was where things got tricky.

She took a deep breath, her mind spinnin' with everything she had to do. The connections she had left were slim. Most people she knew were too scared of Vicente to help her, but there was one person who owed her. Big time.

Johnny "Teflon" Morales. He was known for bein' slippery, able to get his hands on anything for the right price. Fake IDs, guns, drugs—if it was dirty and illegal, Johnny had a way of makin' it happen. And years ago, Nikki had done him a favor that saved his life. Now, it was time to collect.

She picked up her burner phone, the screen cracked from her earlier escape, and dialed his number. The line rang twice before a gravelly voice answered.

"Nikki?" Johnny sounded surprised, and she could hear the suspicion in his tone.

"Yeah, it's me," Nikki said, keepin' her voice low and steady. "I need a favor. And you owe me, Johnny."

A pause. Then, "What you need?"

Nikki took a deep breath. "I need a passport. And it needs to be clean. No traces. No mistakes."

Johnny's laugh crackled through the phone like static. "You know that ain't no small ask, right? Them things ain't easy to come by. And you, Nikki? Word on the street is, you got some real heat on your back."

"I know," she said, her voice hardenin'. "But you owe me, Johnny. Don't forget who saved your ass when everybody else was ready to let you die in the gutter. I need this, or it's over for me."

Another pause. Longer this time. Nikki could practically hear the gears turnin' in his head. He knew helpin' her could get him killed. But he also knew she was right—he owed her.

"Aight, fine," Johnny finally said, his voice low. "But it's gonna cost you."

Nikki's stomach dropped. She barely had anything left. "How much?"

"Ten grand. Cash. And you better have it ready by tomorrow. Meet me at the old docks, near Pier 13."

Nikki gritted her teeth. Ten grand. That was more than she had, but she couldn't afford to let Johnny know she was desperate. "I'll have it."

"Better," Johnny replied, then hung up.

Nikki stared at the phone for a moment, her mind racin'. She didn't have ten grand. Not even close. But there were other ways to get what she needed. She was out of time, out of options, but if there was one thing she knew, it was how to hustle.

The next day, Nikki found herself at one of the underground card games she used to run with back in the day. It wasn't much—a few lowlifes, some middle-tier hustlers, and a couple of drug runners—but it was the only place she could pull in fast cash. She walked in like she still owned the room, even though she felt the weight of every eye on her. People in the game knew Nikki was hot, and they knew gettin' involved with her could mean trouble.

But Nikki wasn't about to let that stop her.

She slid into a chair at the back of the room, pullin' out the last bit of cash she had managed to scrape together. The pot wasn't huge, but it was enough to get her started. She played her hand carefully, lettin' the other players underestimate her. The tension in the room was thick, the kind that made people nervous, but Nikki thrived on it.

By the time the sun started to set, Nikki had doubled her money. But she was still short. And the clock was tickin'.

She pulled out her phone, checkin' the time. She had a couple hours left before the meet with Johnny. She needed more, and there was only one way to get it—by takin' a risk that could either save her or sink her.

When Nikki finally showed up at the old docks, her nerves were on fire. The wind whipped through the empty pier, the smell of saltwater and rust thick in the air. She spotted Johnny waitin' near an old cargo container, his hands in his pockets, a cigarette hangin' from his lips.

"You got the cash?" he asked as she approached, his eyes narrowin' with suspicion.

Nikki nodded, handin' over the bundle of bills. She didn't count it out for him. He'd either take it or leave it.

Johnny glanced down at the money, then back at her. "This better be enough."

"It is," Nikki said, her voice steely. "Now where's my passport?"

Johnny reached into his coat and pulled out a small envelope, handin' it over with a smirk. "This'll get you outta here, no questions asked. But you better move fast. Word is, Vicente's plannin' somethin' big. And you don't wanna be around when it happens."

Nikki snatched the envelope from him, her heart poundin' in her chest. This was it. Her way out. But she still had one more move to make before she could disappear.

The Carnival was in full swing by the time Nikki got back to the city. The streets were flooded with people, music blastin', colors flashin' through the air as dancers and drummers moved through the chaos. It was the perfect cover.

Nikki moved through the crowd like a ghost, her hood pulled low over her face. Every step felt like she was walkin' on the edge of a blade, waitin' for someone to recognize her, to point her out. But the energy of the Carnival kept her hidden, and she used it to her advantage.

She clutched the envelope in her pocket like it was her lifeline, weavin' through the throngs of people. The airport wasn't far, and if she could just make it there without bein' seen, she'd be gone. Free. Vicente would never find her.

But the streets had eyes. And as she passed by a group of men standin' near one of the Carnival floats, she felt it—someone was watchin'. She didn't dare look back, didn't dare make eye contact, but her heart skipped a beat.

They knew.

She picked up her pace, her breath quickenin' as she pushed through the crowd. She could hear the men shoutin', their voices lost in the roar of the Carnival, but she knew they were after her. Vicente's men. Again.

Nikki's legs burned as she ran, her body screamin' for her to stop, but she didn't have time. Not now. She was almost there. Almost free.

But freedom was never easy.

And Nikki was about to find out just how high the price of survival really was.

Chapter 16: Carnival Night

The air was thick with the pulse of drums, the smell of grilled meat, and the scent of sweat mixing with cheap cologne. The streets were alive, bodies swayin' and dancin', the colors of Carnival swirlin' in every direction. But for Nikki, none of the celebration mattered. She was movin' through it all like a shadow, keepin' her head low, her hood up, and her heart racin'.

Every corner felt like a threat. Every side-eye glance, every stranger's smile made her tense up, her body hummin' with the fight-or-flight instinct she had been runnin' on for days. The Carnival was supposed to be a distraction, a perfect cover to slip away. But now, it felt more like a trap, like she was caught in the center of a storm, and any wrong move would have Vicente's men on her in seconds.

She could hear the distant echoes of the steel pan drums, the sharp blasts of horns, and the laughter of people lost in the rhythm of the night. It all blended together, but Nikki's mind was somewhere else. She moved fast, cuttin' through the crowd, her eyes constantly shiftin', lookin' for any sign of danger. She knew they were out there—Vicente's soldiers, waitin', watchin'.

The passport was tucked deep in her pocket, the weight of it heavy against her thigh. It was her way out. Her escape. But with every step, it felt like the streets were closin' in tighter around her.

She ducked into a side alley, tryin' to catch her breath, her hand on the cool brick wall to steady herself. The alley was narrow, the music from the Carnival fading slightly as the dark walls seemed to close in on her. For a moment, it was quiet. Too quiet.

Nikki leaned her head back, eyes closed for a second, tryin' to calm her mind. Her body was on edge, every muscle tense, her heart poundin' in her ears. She needed to stay sharp. This was her last chance. She couldn't afford to slip up.

But then she heard it—a voice, low and familiar. Her eyes snapped open.

"Yo, Nikki! Where you think you goin'?"

Her blood turned to ice.

She turned slowly, her breath catchin' in her throat. A man stepped out from the shadows at the end of the alley, his face hidden under the brim of his baseball cap, his body language casual, but there was a threat in his stance.

"Shit," Nikki muttered under her breath. She recognized him—one of Vicente's lieutenants, always hangin' around in the background, silent but deadly. She hadn't even heard him comin'.

Her mind raced. There was no way to go back into the Carnival crowd without drawin' attention. She was cornered, but her instincts kicked in. She had to keep him talkin', buy herself time.

"I ain't runnin'," she said, her voice steady even though her hands were shakin'. "Just movin' through the streets, same as everybody else tonight. You know how it is."

He smirked, his teeth flashin' in the dim light. "Nah, Nikki. You don't get to move like everybody else no more. Vicente wants to see you. He don't like when people disappear on him."

Nikki's pulse quickened. She was trapped, but she wasn't gonna go down easy. "Tell Vicente if he wants to see me so bad, he can come find me himself."

The man took a step closer, his hand hoverin' near his waist, where she knew he kept his piece. "You can say that when you see him. But you ain't gettin' away this time."

Nikki's body tensed. She could feel the heat risin' in her chest, the fear mixin' with anger. She had worked too hard to get this far, and she wasn't about to let one of Vicente's goons take her down.

Without thinkin', she made her move.

Nikki lunged at him, her fists flyin' toward his face. She wasn't tryin' to take him out—just enough to get him off balance, to buy herself a few precious seconds. He grunted in surprise, stumbling back as her fist connected with his jaw. She could feel the sharp pain in her knuckles, but she didn't stop. She had to move.

Before he could recover, she bolted out of the alley, back into the chaotic flow of the Carnival. Her heart raced as she pushed through the crowd, tryin' to disappear into the sea of bodies dancin' to the music. The man shouted behind her, his voice gettin' lost in the blare of the horns and the beat of the drums.

The streets were alive with energy, but for Nikki, it was all noise, all confusion. She moved quickly, zigzaggin' through the dancers, the air thick with the smell of sweat, smoke, and spilled rum. The colors of the Carnival—bright reds, greens, golds—blurred in her vision as she focused on one thing: escape.

But it wasn't long before she felt it—eyes on her. She turned her head, just for a second, and saw two more of Vicente's men, blendin' into the crowd but headin' straight for her.

Her stomach dropped.

She picked up her pace, her breath comin' in short bursts as she weaved through the revelers, but they were closin' in. Panic clawed at her insides. She couldn't outrun them forever. And there was nowhere to hide.

Nikki darted into another alley, her feet poundin' against the pavement as she ran through the narrow passage. She could hear them behind her now, their footsteps fast and heavy, gettin' closer with every second. She pushed herself harder, her body screamin' for relief, but she didn't stop.

Up ahead, the alley opened up into a side street, and she saw her chance. A group of people were gathered near a food stall, laughin' and shoutin', the smell of jerk chicken fillin' the air. Nikki slid into the crowd, pullin' her hood lower, tryin' to blend in. She could feel her heart beatin' in her throat as she glanced over her shoulder, her eyes dartin' through the crowd.

The men were still lookin', but they hadn't spotted her yet.

For a brief moment, she felt a flicker of hope. Maybe she could still make it. Maybe, just maybe, she could slip through their fingers one last time.

But then, out of the corner of her eye, she saw him. Vicente.

He was standin' across the street, his eyes scanin' the crowd, his face cold, emotionless. He hadn't seen her yet, but Nikki knew it wouldn't take long. His men were circlin', and the net was gettin' tighter.

She was trapped.

Her body tensed, her mind racin'. She could feel the weight of the passport in her pocket, her ticket outta this nightmare. But she had to make it to the airport first. She had to survive the night.

Nikki took a deep breath, her heart poundin'. There was no room for mistakes now. She was runnin' out of time, out of options, but she wasn't ready to give up.

Not yet.

She pushed forward, movin' through the crowd with one goal in mind: freedom.

But freedom came at a price.

And Nikki was about to find out just how high that price was.

Chapter 17: Caught

The night air was thick and suffocating as Nikki made her way toward the docks, her heart pounding like it was about to burst through her chest. The smell of saltwater mixed with the grime of the city, swirling together into a cocktail of fear that clung to her skin. She moved quickly, weaving through the narrow streets, her eyes darting left and right, always looking over her shoulder. Vicente's men were out there, somewhere in the shadows, hunting her down.

But she had made it this far. Just one more step. The boat was waiting.

The plan was simple—get to the docks, board the boat, and be gone before the sun rose. Then she could board a plane out of the Caribbean. She had the fake passport in her pocket, a little cash, and the burning hope that she could finally slip through Vicente's fingers.

But hope was a dangerous thing in a world like hers. It made you believe in miracles that didn't exist.

As she reached the docks, the water lapped against the wooden beams, the distant hum of engines vibrating through the night. She spotted the boat, a small, nondescript fishing vessel. Her ticket out. Her freedom.

Nikki quickened her pace, her legs heavy but her determination stronger. Every nerve in her body was screaming at her to keep moving. Just a few more steps.

But then she heard it.

A voice. Smooth, low, and filled with menace.

"Where you think you goin', Nikki?"

Her heart stopped. Cold dread seeped into her bones as she turned around, the blood draining from her face.

There they were. Vicente's men. Three of them, standing in the shadows, their eyes locked on her like predators sizing up their prey.

The one in the middle, a tall, muscular dude with tattoos running up his neck, stepped forward, a cruel smirk stretching across his face.

Nikki froze. She could feel the world collapsing around her. This was it. She was caught.

"Nah, you ain't goin' nowhere," the man growled, his voice dripping with satisfaction. "Vicente's been lookin' for you, and now... it's time yall had a talk."

Nikki's pulse raced, her eyes darting to the boat. She was so close. So close.

Without thinking, she turned and ran, her feet slamming against the dock, the sound echoing in the night. The men cursed behind her, their footsteps heavy as they gave chase.

Her lungs burned, her legs screaming for relief, but she couldn't stop. She wouldn't stop. Not now. Not when she was this close to freedom.

But freedom was a lie.

One of the men caught up to her, his hand grabbing her by the back of her hoodie, yanking her backward with brutal force. Nikki hit the ground hard, the air knocked out of her lungs as she gasped for breath.

"Thought you could run?" the man snarled, dragging her to her feet as the others closed in. "You really thought you could outrun Vicente?"

Nikki's mind spun, her vision blurry from the impact, but she fought back. She clawed at the man's arms, kicking and thrashing, her nails digging into his skin. But it was no use. He was too strong.

He slammed her against the side of a shipping container, her head snapping back with the force of the blow. Pain shot through her skull, her vision darkening for a moment.

"Stop fightin', Nikki," the man hissed, his face inches from hers. "Ain't no point."

Nikki's chest heaved as she glared at him, her breath ragged. She had been so close. So damn close.

The other two men grabbed her arms, their grip like iron as they forced her to stand. Her body ached, her limbs weak, but her mind was racing. This wasn't how it was supposed to end.

They dragged her across the dock, her feet barely touching the ground as they led her away from the boat. Away from her only chance at escape. She could hear the distant hum of the engine, taunting her, reminding her of the freedom she would never have.

They rounded a corner, and Nikki's heart sank. Standing there, bathed in the dim glow of a streetlamp, was Vicente.

He was calm, collected, like he always was. Dressed sharp in a dark suit, his hands in his pockets, his expression unreadable. But his eyes... his eyes told her everything she needed to know.

This was the end.

Vicente smiled coldly as the men shoved her to the ground in front of him, her knees hitting the concrete with a sickening thud.

"Nikki," he said softly, his voice almost soothing, like a snake before it strikes. "You didn't really think you were gonna get away, did you?"

She stared up at him, her chest heaving, her mind screaming for a way out. But there was none. There never had been.

Vicente stepped closer, his eyes never leaving hers. "You've been runnin' for a long time. But the thing is... you were never in control. You thought you could outsmart me? Play me? Nah, Nikki. You was playin' yourself."

Nikki's throat tightened, her hands trembling as she tried to push herself up, but one of the men kicked her back down, his boot pressing into her spine.

Vicente crouched in front of her, his face inches from hers, his smile widening. "The game was rigged from the start, sweetheart. You were never gonna win."

Nikki clenched her jaw, her body trembling with rage and fear. "You think you're untouchable," she spat, her voice shaky but defiant.

Vicente's smile faded, his eyes darkening. "I know I am."

He stood up, motioning to his men. "Get her up."

They hauled Nikki to her feet again, her body limp in their grasp. She could barely stand, the weight of her failure crushing her.

Vicente circled around her, his presence suffocating. "You could've had it all, Nikki. You were smart. But you thought you could play in a game you didn't understand. And now... you gotta pay."

Nikki's chest tightened, tears stinging the corners of her eyes. She had thought she could outsmart him. Thought she could win. But Vicente had been two steps ahead the whole time. And now, she was out of moves.

"Take her to the spot," Vicente said, his voice cold and final. "Make sure she knows what happens when you cross me."

The men dragged her toward a black SUV parked nearby, her body too weak to resist. She could hear the distant echoes of the Carnival, the music, the laughter... but it all felt so far away now. Like another life. A life she would never have.

As they threw her into the back of the SUV, Nikki's mind was racing. She had fought so hard, clawed her way through every obstacle, but in the end... the streets had won.

And now, she was about to pay the ultimate price.

The door slammed shut, sealing her fate.

And as the SUV roared to life, driving off into the night, Nikki knew one thing for sure.

There was no escape.

Not from Vicente.

Not from the streets.

And not from herself.

Chapter 18: The Final Confrontation

The SUV rattled over the cracked streets, headlights slicing through the darkness like knives. Nikki lay in the back seat, her hands bound, wrists raw from the rough rope, and her body aching from the fight. Her chest was tight, each breath shallow as fear gripped her. She knew this was it—her final ride. Vicente wasn't bringin' her in for a chat. He was done playin' games.

As they drove through the city, the sounds of the Carnival grew fainter. The music, the laughter, the life she'd been running from—it was all slipping away, just like the last shreds of hope she had left. Nikki tried to shift her body, the ropes diggin' into her skin, her muscles burnin', but she couldn't move much. She glanced out the tinted window at the passing buildings, her mind racing. She had to think of somethin'. Fast.

They pulled up to an old, abandoned warehouse on the outskirts of town, the kind of place where people disappeared and never came back. The kind of place where endings were written in blood.

Vicente was already there, leanin' against the hood of his sleek black car, arms crossed, his face expressionless. His men dragged Nikki out of the SUV, tossin' her to the ground like a piece of trash. The gravel bit into her knees, but she forced herself to stand, her breath catchin' in her throat.

She stared at Vicente, her heart hammerin' in her chest. He looked calm, collected, like this was just another day at the office for him. But there was somethin' colder in his eyes tonight. Somethin' final.

He nodded to his men, and they stepped back, givin' the two of them space. Nikki knew what this was—her last chance. The game was over, and she was out of moves. But if there was one thing Nikki knew how to do, it was talk her way outta trouble.

She had done it a thousand times before.

"Vicente," she started, her voice shaky but steady enough. "You don't have to do this. I get it. I messed up. But we can fix this. I can still be useful to you. I got connections. I can make you more money than you've ever seen before."

Vicente stared at her, his face unreadable. He didn't say a word, but his silence was louder than any threat he could've made. Nikki felt her stomach twist.

She tried again, takin' a step closer. "Look, I ain't tryin' to disrespect you. I know you run this shit. I know you always been ten steps ahead. I was stupid for thinkin' I could outplay you. But you gotta understand—this ain't gotta be the end. We can work somethin' out."

Vicente finally spoke, his voice low and calm, but each word felt like a bullet. "Nikki, you been runnin' game for too long. You think you can talk your way out of anything. But that's your problem. You talk too much."

Nikki's chest tightened. She could feel the ground slippin' out from under her. But she wasn't done yet. "I know you don't trust me, and I get that. But I can fix this. I can get you what you need. Just give me a chance. I ain't askin' for much, just one more shot."

Vicente shook his head, his eyes cold. "You don't get it, do you? You already had your shot. You had more than enough chances to prove yourself. And every time, you fucked up. This ain't about money anymore, Nikki. This is about loyalty. You broke that."

Nikki felt the tears burnin' at the back of her eyes, but she swallowed them down. She couldn't break. Not in front of him. "Vicente, please. I'm beggin' you. You don't gotta do this. I'll disappear. You'll never see me again. I swear."

Vicente took a step forward, his presence heavy and suffocating. He was close enough now that Nikki could feel the weight of his gaze, the finality in his movements. "You think this is about lettin' you go? Nah, Nikki. This is about makin' sure nobody else even thinks about crossin' me like you did."

She tried to hold his stare, tried to stay strong, but her body was tremblin'. She could feel the end comin', could feel it in the way Vicente's men stood watchin', their hands on their guns, waitin' for the order.

"I trusted you," Vicente said, his voice quieter now, almost thoughtful. "You coulda been somethin'. But you thought you could outsmart me, thought you could run."

Nikki shook her head, her voice barely a whisper. "I didn't want this."

"But you brought it on yourself," Vicente finished, his eyes hardenin'. "This is the streets, Nikki. And the streets don't let nobody walk away."

She opened her mouth to say somethin'—anything—but the words wouldn't come. Vicente turned his back on her, motioning to his men. Nikki's heart raced as the two men grabbed her, pullin' her toward the back of the warehouse. Her legs felt like lead, her body numb, but she fought against them, panic settin' in.

"Wait! Vicente, please! You don't have to do this!" she screamed, her voice crackin'. She struggled, her body jerkin' as she tried to break free, but it was no use. The men were too strong, too determined.

Vicente didn't even turn around. He just stood there, his back to her, hands in his pockets, as they dragged her away.

Nikki's mind raced. This couldn't be how it ended. She had fought too hard, survived too much to go out like this. But deep down, she knew it was over. The game had been rigged from the start.

They threw her to the ground, the cold concrete biting into her skin. One of the men pulled out a gun, his expression blank, like this was just another task. Another job. Nikki's chest tightened, her breath shallow as she stared up at the barrel of the gun, the cold metal gleaming in the dim light.

This was it.

She tried to fight the panic, tried to hold on to the last bit of control she had left, but it was slipping away. She had always been the one in control, always the one finessin' her way out of tight spots, but now? Now she was just another casualty of the streets.

The man raised the gun, and Nikki closed her eyes, her heart poundin' so loud it drowned out everything else. She could hear the distant sounds of the Carnival, the music, the laughter, all of it so far away. Like another world. A world she'd never see again.

"Do it," Vicente's voice came from the distance, cold and final.

Nikki's breath hitched.

And then, the gunshot.

The sound echoed through the empty warehouse, a single, deafening crack that cut through the night.

Nikki's body jerked, and for a split second, everything went silent. Cold. Numb.

And then... darkness.

Chapter 19: The End

The gunshot echoed in Nikki's ears, her whole world reduced to a single, deafening sound. She waited for the pain, the sharp bite of the bullet that would end it all. Her breath caught in her throat, her body frozen in anticipation of death. But nothing happened.

The cold concrete pressed against her cheek, rough and unforgiving, and the distant hum of the Carnival floated through the night like a twisted reminder of life continuing just beyond her reach. Her heart raced, but there was no blood, no explosion of agony. Just a warning shot some torture foreplay.

She blinked, confusion flooding her mind, and dared to open her eyes. The man who had been aiming the gun stood still, his arm lowered, and his eyes fixed on something behind her. The gun wasn't pointed at her anymore.

The air shifted, tense and cracklin' with somethin' new, somethin' dangerous.

Footsteps echoed behind her, slow and deliberate, like someone who wasn't in a hurry. Nikki twisted her neck to see who it was, her heart pounding in her chest like a trapped animal. And then she saw him.

Rome.

For a split second, relief washed over her. He had come for her. He hadn't left her to die. Rome was gonna save her, just like he always did, when things got too hot, when the streets threatened to swallow her whole. But then... somethin' about his face. His expression. It wasn't relief, or fear, or even anger. It was calm. Too calm.

"Nikki," Rome's voice cut through the thick night air, smooth as ever, but cold. Cold like ice water runnin' through her veins. "You really thought you could pull one over on us?"

Her heart stuttered, her breath catchin' in her throat. *On us?* The words hit her like a punch to the gut.

"What... what the fuck you talkin' 'bout, Rome?" Her voice came out broken, shaky. She could barely get the words out, but she needed answers.

Rome stepped closer, the shadows from the streetlamp dancin' on his face, half in light, half in darkness. Behind him, Vicente watched, his arms crossed, a satisfied smirk stretchin' across his face. The pieces of the puzzle were comin' together too fast for Nikki to process, but she could feel the betrayal settlin' in, like a knife twistin' in her chest.

"Nikki," Rome said, almost like he was disappointed in her, like she was a kid who messed up real bad. "You always thought you was smarter than everybody else. Always thought you could play the game and win. But you never realized—you wasn't the one runnin' it."

Nikki's body trembled as the truth began to sink in, the full weight of what was happenin' crushin' her from the inside. "Nah, Rome. You lyin'. You... you said you loved me. We... we was in this together."

Rome chuckled, but it was hollow, empty. There was no warmth in it. "Yeah, I told you what you needed to hear. I played my part. But this ain't no love story, Nikki. This is business. And you? You was always just part of the plan."

She felt like the ground had been ripped from under her. She was fallin', spiralin', her whole world crashin' down. He was in on it. The whole time.

All those nights she spent with him, thinkin' he was her escape, her way outta the mess. All those promises. Lies. It was all a setup. Vicente's men, the chases, the close calls... all part of the game they had been playin' with her.

Nikki shook her head, her voice crackin' with disbelief. "You... you used me, Rome? After everything? All the shit we been through?"

Rome didn't even flinch. "Used you? Nah, Nikki. I put you where you needed to be. You did your job, and now it's done. That's all it was."

Tears stung Nikki's eyes, but she refused to let them fall. Not in front of them. Not in front of Vicente, who stood there, enjoyin' the show, like he knew this was how it was always gonna end. Like he knew she was never gonna win.

Vicente stepped forward now, that sick smirk still plastered on his face. "I gotta hand it to you, Nikki. You put up a good fight. I ain't seen nobody hustle like you in a minute. But like Rome said... you was never in control."

Nikki's chest tightened. She felt like she couldn't breathe, like the weight of everything was pressin' down on her all at once. She tried to speak, but the words were caught in her throat.

Rome bent down, grabbin' her by the chin, his face close enough that she could feel his breath on her skin. "You thought you could outsmart Vicente? Outsmart me? Baby, you don't even know how deep this shit goes."

Her body went numb. Everything she'd done, every move she'd made... it had all been part of their game. They'd been usin' her from the start.

"Why?" Nikki whispered, her voice barely audible. "Why would you do this to me?"

Rome's eyes darkened, his grip tightenin' on her chin. "Because there's no room for someone like you at the top. You ain't built for this. And now... you're just a loose end."

The pain in Nikki's chest was unbearable. This was worse than any gunshot, worse than any street fight she'd ever been in. The man she trusted, the one she thought she could count on, had been the one to betray her. The one to destroy her.

She glared at Rome, her voice filled with venom. "I shoulda known. You ain't never been nothin' but a snake. Both of y'all."

Rome stood up, lettin' go of her chin, his expression hardenin'. "That's where you fucked up, Nikki. You always thought you was different. Special. But you ain't. You're just like everybody else who thought they could win this game."

Vicente nodded to his men, and they moved in closer, their eyes gleamin' with cold intent. Nikki knew what was comin'. There was no talkin' her way out of this one. No more chances. No more moves.

She had been playin' a game she didn't even know existed.

Vicente stepped up to her, his voice low, but every word cut like a blade. "You made too many mistakes, Nikki. You thought you was playin' us, but you was the one gettin' played. Now, there's only one way this ends."

The man with the gun stepped forward again, the barrel glintin' in the dim light. Nikki's heart raced, her mind screamin' for some kind of miracle, some way out. But she knew... this was it.

Rome's voice echoed in her ears as he took a step back, his face emotionless. "This is just business, Nikki. Nothing personal."

Nikki's breath came out in ragged gasps as the cold realization settled in. This was how it ended. Not with a bang, but with betrayal. She had been fooled by a man who said he loved her, twisted and turned in a game she never stood a chance in.

And now, she was payin' the price.

The gun was raised again, the barrel pointed at her chest.

Vicente nodded.

And then... the sound of the trigger being pulled.

Nikki didn't flinch this time. She was done runnin'.

Chapter 20: The Final Mas

The harbor water lapped against the dock, its murky surface calm, undisturbed by the chaos that had unfolded in the streets the night before. Early morning light peeked through the clouds, casting a dim glow over the city. But today wasn't like any other day. The streets were already buzzin', voices hushed but filled with shock, curiosity, and fear.

Nikki's body had been found.

She floated just beneath the surface, her arms limp, her once-vibrant face hidden behind a Carnival mask. A mockery of the woman she had been. Her body drifted there like an empty shell, nothin' but a memory, a ghost in the city she had tried so hard to escape.

The news spread like wildfire. Word on the streets was that Nikki had crossed the wrong people. The same whispers that had once praised her hustle, her beauty, and her charm were now filled with dark amusement, as if everyone had seen it comin'. "She flew too close to the sun," they said. "You can't mess with the game and expect to walk away."

A crowd gathered near the harbor, watchin' as the police fished her out of the water. The officers didn't seem too interested, barely lookin' at her like she was just another body they'd seen a hundred times before. In the end, she was just another statistic. Another girl who thought she could survive the streets but found out too late that the streets always win.

As the onlookers whispered, speculatin' about what had happened, one man stood at the back of the crowd, hands in his pockets, his expression unreadable. Rome. He watched in silence as the police hauled Nikki's body up onto the dock. Her stoic face coverin' the truth of what had happened the night before.

Rome's eyes didn't show no sadness. No regret. He was calm, collected, just like always. He had played his part, and now the game was over. Nikki was gone, and he walked away without a scratch. That's how it was supposed to be. That's how it always ended for people like him.

He turned his back on the scene, walkin' away as the streets kept buzzin' around him, the voices loud but distant in his mind. People would talk for a while, sure. There'd be rumors, theories, but none of it mattered. He and Vicente had cleaned it up nice and neat. Nobody would ever know the real story. To the streets, Nikki was just another girl who got in over her head.

The whispers spread fast, faster than Nikki had ever moved through the city. People in the streets were already speculatin', piecin' together what little they knew.

"I heard she tried to run off with some drug money," one man said, leanin' back in his chair as he got his cut.

"Nah, bro, she was tryna take over Vicente's game," another guy chimed in, shakin' his head. "She was gettin' too bold."

The women at the salon had their own version of the story, the gossip flowin' thick.

"Girl, I heard she was messin' with Rome behind Vicente's back."

"Nah, sis. She was playin' both of 'em. Thought she was slick."

The truth? That was lost in the noise. No one really knew what had happened, and no one ever would. But they all knew one thing—Nikki had been playin' with fire, and now she was burnin'.

Vicente's name stayed clean. Untouchable. That's how he'd always kept it. And Rome? He was the street legend now, a shadow that moved in the dark, never gettin' caught, never takin' the fall. They'd set Nikki up perfectly, played her like a fiddle, and when her usefulness had run out, they tossed her aside without a second thought.

The Carnival still pulsed in the distance, the colors, the music, the celebration of life contrastin' with the body now floatin' in the harbor. But for Nikki? The masquerade was over. The mask, once a symbol of seduction and power, had now become her death shroud.

The old heads on the block had seen this kind of story play out a thousand times. They stood on the corner, smokin' and watchin' the city move, the youngins passin' by, unaware of the traps that were laid in front of them.

"You see what happened to that girl Nikki?" one of the older men asked, his voice raspy from too many years of cigarettes and cheap liquor.

The others nodded, shakin' their heads. "Yeah, man. You can never really win when you play the game."

A pause, then the old man added, "Ain't nobody ever been smart enough for these streets. Not in the long run."

They all knew it. Everybody did. The streets didn't care about how slick you were, how pretty or how smart. The streets had one rule—survive or get swallowed whole. And Nikki? She had been swallowed, chewed up, and spit out.

That night, the Carnival went on as planned. The lights glittered, the people danced, and the music filled the air with life. But if you listened closely, beneath the drum beats and the laughter, you could hear the whispers.

"Nikki's gone."

"They found her floatin' in the harbor."

And like that, Nikki became a legend. Not the kind of legend she had wanted to be. Not the story of a girl who made it out, who rose to the top. No. She became a warning. A cautionary tale whispered among the hustlers, the dancers, the dreamers.

And maybe that was the most tragic part of it all. Nikki had played the game as hard as she could, but in the end, the game had played her. The streets always had the final say.

As the night deepened and the city pulsed with life, Vicente and Rome sat in a private room at the back of a club, glasses raised, their faces shadowed by the dim light. They didn't talk about Nikki. They didn't need to.

And outside, the Carnival roared on, the streets vibratin' with music and life, as if nothin' had happened. As if Nikki had never existed.

Don't miss out!

Visit the website below and you can sign up to receive emails whenever Rachael Reed publishes a new book. There's no charge and no obligation.

https://books2read.com/r/B-A-WXARB-XYQBF

BOOKS 2 READ

Connecting independent readers to independent writers.

Did you love *Caribbean Carnival Hoe*? Then you should read *Can't Turn a Hoe Into a Housewife*[1] by Rachael Reed!

[2]

In the gritty streets of the city, where loyalty is tested and danger lurks around every corner, Can't Turn a Hoe into a Housewife dives deep into the underbelly of urban life. Erica, a seasoned escort with a sharp mind and a guarded heart, dreams of escaping the fast life and finding something real. But in a world where money rules and trust is scarce, her journey ain't easy.

When Erica crosses paths with Quan, a man with a genuine heart and a promise of love, she sees a glimmer of hope. But leaving the game ain't simple, especially with a ruthless pimp like Lil Ron, who ain't about to let his top girl go without a fight. As Erica tries to walk the line

---

1. https://books2read.com/u/4XdEN1

2. https://books2read.com/u/4XdEN1

between her old life and a new beginning, Lil Ron tightens his grip, turning their lives into a deadly game of cat and mouse.

Can't Turn a Hoe into a Housewife is a tale of love, betrayal, and survival in a world where the streets don't play fair. With a dark, raw tone and a cast of characters struggling against their circumstances, this story is packed with twists, drama, and the harsh reality of street life. As Erica fights to break free and find redemption, the stakes get higher, and the danger becomes all too real.

In this urban fiction thriller, the line between right and wrong blurs, and every choice comes with a price. Will Erica escape the life that's bound her, or will the streets claim her for good? Get ready for a cliffhanging ride through the hood, where love ain't always enough to save you from your past.

Also by Rachael Reed

Sis
Sis 2 Blood on the Streets

Standalone
Codefendant
Codefendant
Once a Cheater
Once a Cheater
Passport Bro
What Happens in Prison
Preference
Sprinkle Sprinkle
Championship Bad
Street Exodus
Street Exodus
Street Royalty
Pawns of Power
SIS
Cartel Bloodline
Get Money Girls
Skip the Games
Til Death Do Us Part

Backpage Hustle
Link in Bio
The Virgin and The Kingpin
A Gangsta's Heart
Boosters
Can't Turn a Hoe Into a Housewife
Better you Than Me
Wig Dealer: How to Start Your wig Business
Trail Ride Blues
Demure Diva
Queen of the Carnival
Caribbean Carnival Hoe